About the author

Pippa Bartolotti has been writing her whole life.
An enthusiastic letter writer as a child, she soon
made human rights and climate change her
specialist subjects. She has been a successful
business entrepreneur, Green Party Leader in
Wales and extensive traveler. She is now intent
on committing her vast store of knowledge into
readable fiction. *Barbarian* is her fifth book.

BARBARIAN

Pippa Bartolotti

BARBARIAN

Vanguard Press

A CIP catalogue record for this title is
available from the British Library.

ISBN 978 1 784655 79 2

*Vanguard Press is an imprint of
Pegasus Elliot MacKenzie Publishers Ltd.*
www.pegasuspublishers.com

First Published in 2019

**Vanguard Press
Sheraton House Castle Park
Cambridge England**

Printed & Bound in Great Britain

Dedication

The Bishnois consider trees as sacred, but their empathy extends to every living being on earth. The spirit of conservation has been deeply ingrained in every Brishnoi for over five centuries. It arises from the belief that every living organism on this earth has an equal right to live.

I dedicate this book to the Bishnoi of Rajasthan, who by thought, word and deed have committed their many generations to protection of the environment – at times giving up their lives.

What Was and What Is

"Was it utopia?"

The teenager was suffocating under the putrid smell of discarded blankets. Dirty, frayed, with suspicious yellow stains; home comforts stitched together with the bitter threads of irony; no home, no comfort. Home oxymorons maybe. Her flame red hair was stuffed unceremoniously under someone else's tweed cap. It might have been tweed, no-one cared. It looked ludicrously perky considering their situation. She was addressing her grandmother, who had been telling stories of days she couldn't quite remember. Days when the shops were crowded with food, when the lights came on, when you could travel anywhere on the planet. They might have been true.

The two women huddled together near the pock-marked hearth of what once had been an average middle-class sitting room. There were remnants of floor tiles but scant furniture – you could include rusting metal legs which might have belonged to a chair as furniture, up to you. A carved mahogany mirror was incongruously embedded over what might have been the mantelpiece. It stared desperation back at them. The grimy stove meted out a reluctant light, and an even fainter heat, but it was more than some people had, and anyway, they did not want to draw attention to themselves. Barwin drew her feet closer to her body. It was a bad time for extremities.

"I suppose it was a kind of utopia," said the grandmother, hesitant amid her clamouring thoughts, unable to decipher most of them. "We tended to think that better living was just around the corner. It was probably the nearest we ever got to utopia. We were having a lot of fun."

She fell back into a cavorting haze of dazzling lights, fashionable clothes, and tables heavy with food. Gaiety percolated in happy bubbles from the imagined past to keep her company. The corners of her mouth curled up, just a little, and her pale blue eyes twinkled, gently reflecting the tiny sapphire earrings she swore she would rather die for than give up. "A girl has to have standards," she had chuckled when she was asked to part with them for a few groceries. The old lady would remain unmoved on this subject no matter the hardships facing them. She had lost, or sold, almost everything she had ever owned, but those earrings were staying put.

The wind changed direction and swirled belligerently round the house. An icy north-easterly. The temperature dropped, and the two women drew closer together. The older woman lost in the effervescent past of plenty, the younger one considering the future. If there was one.

Shots rang out in the distance, interrupting the grandmother from her reverie. "Did you find any bullets for that old gun, Bar?"

"No, Gran, but I found a couple of damaged stab-proof vests the other day. I reckon I can stitch them up to make one decent garment."

They didn't need to discuss how exactly the 'damaged' vests had come into Barwin's hands. The shifting sands of power on the streets led to daily casualties; both knew that tearing a can of beans from a dying woman's hand was the sensible thing to do. If you stopped to think about it… well, you didn't. Another scavenger would beat you to it. Godless? Who knew. If anyone's God was still around, most would meet him sooner rather than later. Choose a dead morality or a living hell. Anyone?

The still winter night could not carry the smell of wood-smoke away. Some chilly nights, when the guttural shrieks of marauding voices paralysed every sinew, they would sit in shrinking cold. Being found was as good as being dead, but less comfortable.

Their food was stacked in a rudimentary cellar Barwin had been digging out under the floorboards of a downstairs room. It was more of a pit in truth, and Barwin, terrified of losing her hard-won tins of miscellany, laboriously dug it out every time she added something which they could not eat in a day, and packed the earth down tight afterwards, replacing the floorboards, then rubbing earth into the cracks, stamping manically over the scene, the crime scene, the scene of forbidden surplus. Energy wasted to protect potential energy gain. There must be a formula for that.

Losing, or finding food had become, quite literally, her reason for being. If they had to leave the house in a hurry, she could come back and retrieve the food if it was hidden well enough. There was no formula for that, unless $F=$ Fear, or maybe Famine, or both. Mathematics is unrepentant.

They had happened to this house, on the bleak outskirts of town, when their own suburb had been ransacked. The initial plan had been to go back to the previous place when the commotion died down, but the houses burned for days. Barwin didn't want to go back, and her grandmother, in her more lucid moments, knew that nothing would be as it had been. They would probably have to move on again in any case.

The current house, although damaged, was quite old. It still had shutters, which were important for keeping out any light from inside. It might have been important for keeping heat in, but they never seemed to create enough of that beyond a couple of feet from the stove, so the thought was laughably academic. The shutters had been painted stuck in years gone by. It was a small task to knife the layers of paint away and get them working again. Miraculously, this house had that wondrous gift of an otherwise belligerent universe – a stove – and some pots and pans, which you couldn't eat, but were extremely useful for boiling water and scavenged food. Yes, food was the main preoccupation.

An underground culvert had run beside the house to take water from a small stream away. That was the best thing about old houses, there was usually a water supply close by. Barwin had broken through the concrete shell, and with judicious use of a chipped lidless teapot and a piece of hose jammed onto the spout, could collect fresh water. A surprise luxury. As the house was on a hill, the spring water was relatively clean - a huge improvement on their last staging post where she suspected the underground brook was contaminated with all manner of revolting detritus. She had fished out a dead cat herself, rotting among the decaying plastic which choked most watercourses. Poor emaciated thing. She could only pity the once domesticated animals now forced to fend for themselves. She could not give them what they needed most – food. They were all scavengers together. Now. There was only now, the moment, the present, the here and now. For the cat it had been then.

If times had been hard in past years, they were as nothing compared to now, the present, this moment. Man-made laws are changeable and shifting; the laws of physics are fixed. The sea had continued to rise, and coastal communities had been all but wiped out by the increasing ferocity of storms. The oceans spumed plastic spittle as gales contorted the land and the sea into a ferocious clutter so twisted you could barely tell the difference between them. Cartographers drew and redrew their blasted maps. After every storm there was a little more sea, a little less land. Maybe somewhere else it was the other way round. But they weren't somewhere else. People salvaged what they could, built flimsy shelters, moved to higher ground, but there wasn't enough fertile land to feed everyone, and the ability to tease life back into depleted soil rested with time – the belligerent child of need, the master and mistress of them all. In any case, she hadn't seen a bee since her childhood, so pollination had to be done by hand, and that only made sense if you were going to stick around long enough to reap the harvest.

The sedentary economy was dead. The economy was dead, over, kaput. The flimsy roofs of call centres rotted into the ground and their tangled wrecks conjoined with out-of-town shopping malls. Ashes to ashes, dust to dust. And it was hardly the dawn of the new hunter gatherers either – unless you want to classify frightened scavengers as the epoch following the Anthropocene. Well, that didn't last long, did it. What a come down.

Her mother had known.

The passivity of nature had presented a false image of herself. Like a woman defiled she was too much in shock to react effectively, at first. The delay had lulled humans into a sense of false security, and they continued to think they had divine right, because a story book written a thousand years ago said so, and men took the story as truth. They thought they should take dominion over the fish of the sea, and over the fowl of the air, and over the cattle, and over all the earth, and over every creeping thing that creepeth upon the earth, and in their childish wilfulness they saw no consequence. When the first coal-fired power station began to belch its poison into the air, there was no hurricane to put them right. Nature decided it was the foolish play of a toddler, and the toddler would grow up and take responsibility for its own actions. But the child continued its reckless play because it got affirmation, not in the form of anything natural, but in the form of pieces of metal coins, devised by man as a convenience for exchange, but even that was not enough. The pieces of metal became an end in themselves, and to get more of them, nature had to suffer more.

For a hundred years she suffered, her atmosphere poisoned, her land stripped, her non-human children tortured to extinction. They moved on, tried to adapt, but time and again they were exterminated as their homes and habitats were razed to the ground.

The pieces of metal were replaced by computer digits, and still people wanted more of them. The great psychological marketing swindle of the twentieth century devised a constant barrage of propaganda. Everyone should want more of everything, and they should want it now, even if they could not afford it. More of everything meant more mining, more deforestation, more poisons. Nature started to pack her bags. If humans could not control themselves, she would assert herself, and there would be no compromises.

Barwin had painstakingly pollinated the apple flowers in a small orchard in her original home with a feather tied to a stick. She clung on to the hope that they could stay there long enough to gather the apples, but the gangs had come, she and her grandmother had to leave quickly just to stay alive. Barwin crept back a few months later, but to her horror the trees had been chopped down, probably for firewood. The short-sightedness and ignorance of these gangs hurt her to the core. They probably had no idea that apples grew on trees.

Gone were the big dreams of mechanisation taking the work out of work. The technicians were too busy hunting for food to worry about their automatons. Everything had to be done by hand, if it could be done at all. The factories had closed down and been pillaged; the cities were crumbling. Iconic erections to human pride echoed only to the moaning of the wind.

She could not remember the time that the polar bears became extinct. That had happened in her mother's time. But she grew up knowing about the warming, experiencing the warming. Warm seas fuel hurricanes, warm air bloats with water vapour, the rising sea encroaches on the land. The consequences of tiny random acts of thoughtless consumerism echoed throughout the world. She grew up hungry. It was not through poverty. It was because they could never seem to grow enough food. Crops were parched or washed away. The seasons ducked and dived like a mythical dragon, wounded and angry. The loss of the polar bears had barely created a ripple in the news. Her mother had told her that so many species had been lost already that just one more on the list made little or no difference. Nature had packed her bags and she was leaving.

The voice of her mother often came back to Barwin. Her mother had known what would happen, and along with a few dedicated scientists had tried to warn the world, the governments, industry, in fact anyone who would listen. They listened all right, but did nothing. Everything could have been done, and they chose to do nothing. The corporations had become bigger than countries – in some cases bigger than continents. Their sole purpose was profit. Billionaires, tyrants and oligarchs had bought elections and twisted democracy to their will. Governments became powerless to act in the interests of any other body but the corporations. And so the burning was barely abated, the land continued to be punished with too many artificial fertilizers, the food continued to be contaminated with pesticides, hormones and antibiotics. Her mother had died at the largest anti-capitalist protest the country had ever seen. Shot dead, point blank range, they said, in the face. She died trying to protect the future. Many did, that day.

The police weren't there to protect the people, they were there to protect the profits. So were the army, staked out in their sandbags around the big banks, they took aim at the people. Just following orders, they said, washing their collective hands in the collecting bowl of shame. And the shooting continued, day after day, and the mounting bodies spoke louder than the guns, and it was all too late anyway.

"Three days, can't be…" muttered her grandmother, propped up with blankets and assorted coordinated home furnishings debris in the fading glow of the fire. What was left of the 'home furnishings' bore the grubby label of a smart city department store, long looted, long gone. All the pomp and pretentiousness of the bourgeoisie reduced to a few rags, tattered smelly rags, with a smart and utterly useless label, just like the middle classes themselves, what was left of them, still carrying their labels and making sure they held their knives and forks properly as they sat round the table eating their invisible meal, and the TV flickered off, for the last time, cutting the cocaine-riddled game show host off in mid-question, mid-life, his sorry prime, time. They would never know the answer to the superfluous question. The uneducated did better. They did not even know the question.

The old lady was sleeping fitfully now, her breathing laboured. Barwin gently moved her head so that she could rest more easily.

"Three days," Barwin mused. "Maybe that was the start of it. Only three days food supply in any given city."

It wasn't the start of it, but it was the first real manifestation of the instability of everyday life. The authorities kept the latent insecurity in the system well hidden. Disguised as a 'just in time' policy, it would become a 'just too late' reality. For so long people had taken food and clothing for granted. They bought more than they needed and threw the surplus away, having absolutely no concept of the vast amount of resources needed to make the stuff they discarded.

Vegetables were transported across continents when they could be grown in a field near home, the carbon created by air travel unseen, uncounted. The stripping of natural forest for palm oil plantations, unseen, uncounted. The gentle orangutans who tried to fight the bulldozers unseen, uncounted. The dairy cows who would never see the light of day, unseen, uncounted. The list went on forever. Violation piled on top of violation, cruelty bred more cruelty and the interminable cycle spun on and on as the human population increased on the back of misplaced trust that 'the system' would continue to deliver.

And the persistence of the patriarchal system did not deliver. A few shillings were handed out to those few who couldn't find their place in the shiny new society of abusive plenty, and for the most part they conveniently died of cold in the shuttered shop doorways of the retail palaces.

The storms continued to intensify, the seasons retreated in confusion. It was the dawning of the paradox of an abundant yet unequal world giving rise to the grim equality of nothing.

Nobody saw the last bee die, and in the space of one harvest, the price of a Golden Delicious apple rose to the price of gold. Suddenly nobody needed gold. Some prayed – as if they had not sinned enough.

Within six months the farms had to convert to growing wheat, oats and corn, clothing became in short supply as the cotton plants were no longer pollinated, plant oils used for fuel consumed the rainforests.

Despite the push for energy sources based on the natural flows of nature, the system was far too dependent on bio fuels. Edible crops were concentrated in too few seed varieties owned by a handful of corporations, and much of the seed was designed to be sterile, ensuring a regular and abhorrent income for those who seldom needed it. Untold billions were given to the corporations to promote unhealthy and unwise products, products which denuded the ancient rainforests of their viability, wasting prodigious quantities of water and nutrients as if the source was infinite.

Human diet became ever more restricted. Only crops which transported well were bred, largely devoid of the minerals and natural medicines a varied diet would provide. Emergent nations demanded ever more meat to eat, wasting yet more water and yet more food. Cattle and poultry were rammed into dingy sheds, their sentience forgotten in the reckless ambition to produce more and more meat. Overcrowding and the introduction of growth hormones gave rise to sickness, and the cycle of health buckled under the strain. Increased use of antibiotics gave rise to resistant strains of bacteria and the writing was on the wall, except that few cared enough to read it.

It was probably the triple whammy which marked the change of everything. The massive hurricane of 2029, the overcrowding in towns and cities, and the ongoing epidemic of Mallavirus, released from the melting Russian permafrost. They were warned, it was expected, there was no cure, there was no contingency.

Hurricane Angelo unleashed its horrors over almost a quarter of the globe, killed and maimed hundreds of thousands, millions maybe, devastated towns and cities and all but destroyed the energy and communications networks. Huge atmospheric rivers of moist air were reported coming their way. It was one of the last news reports Barwin ever heard, back then, just eight years old, watching the taut faces of her family gathering slowly round the computer newsfeed. Roads were suddenly impassable, mudslides enraged the floods, and if any crops had survived the onslaught, they could not be transported over broken roads.

It was common knowledge that if there was any interruption in the food system, in three short day's there would be empty shelves in the shops. At no time in history had so many people lived more than one days walk from where any food is produced.

Those tittering on the precarious line of impoverishment were the first to suffer. They had little in the way of food stocks to fall back on. Of course they ransacked the shops, the streets, the factories – they were hungry. Law and order became as extinct as the polar bear.

Hospitals, already struggling to cope with the new virus epidemic, lost the fight almost as soon as they lost power supplies. Doctors and nurses worked wherever they could, however they could, but they were fighting shadows. They slowly ran out of medicines, pain killers, even disinfectants, and the hospitals which escaped catastrophic damage from the hurricane became shelters for those who had lost everything, but even they had to abandon the city in their search for food.

Only the rich, yes, they knew. Simultaneously they grasped at everything and made everything worse. They sucked the money out of the society which made them, gated themselves behind wisteria walls and razor wire, bought the law and abandoned the order, filled their underground warehouses and their estates with weapons, private armies, and the bounty of a generation. The rich planned to survive, at all costs.

"Ah well, "sighed Barwin, "we are where we are." And she settled down next to her grandmother to sleep.

Barwin was no street-fighter, but she was resourceful. She was short in stature, should have been plump as a pillow, homely you might say, in nature too, but this was not the time for girlish whims or female comforts. The womanly figure which might be, was as skinny as a dead cat, but what hadn't fed her body had fed her mind. She thought deeply about the tasks in hand, she watched others, and she used her brain to overcome obstacles which might defeat a person with more brawn. In this way she had survived. A nature welded to survival, every minute, every day, instinctive, careful, strategic.

Sebastian

Breakfast was a solid affair of oats and rice from the night before. Solid enough to fill you, and nutritious enough to keep you alive. It was boring, but in the absence of pollinators it was pretty much all you could get unless you got lucky. At least there was water.

Barwin had been examining the thought of leaving her grandmother to scout more of the surrounding countryside. She knew that somewhere out there the wealthiest people might still be hiding food which would most probably have been stockpiled from more abundant days. It was true that even their supplies would have been depleted in the four years since Angelo, but whilst hope lives with every next breath, the life-force, and the will to survive is stronger still.

It was not hope which motivated her, which in many ways is as good as sitting down praying, it was the need to use every day productively, to forage for survival, for a day wasted was a day lost, or even a life. The value of all life was the essence of her being. Her parents had instilled in her a deep respect and compassion for all living things. They had never caused an animal to be killed on their behalf, not eaten one since they were old enough to make decisions, and as a result Barwin did not even know what meat tasted like. She had never looked at a piece of meat as anything other than a symbol of cruelty, and the family had come to regard all dairy products in a similar vein. Taking a calf from its mother at one day old so that humans could have the milk for themselves seemed to her to be an outrageous flagrance of natural laws, the result of which did little more than salve the taste buds of people who had already become conditioned by incessant marketing to think of animal milk as good for them.

Before setting off once more into the eternal unknown, she had to find the right place in which to install her grandmother. She resolved to go out that morning to make a preliminary reconnoitre of the immediate terrain.

Reluctantly removing the blanket from her shoulders, she made a mental note to dig up a grave if necessary, for more clothing, stuffed some escaping strands of neon hair back into her cap, and announced to her vaguely understanding grandmother the plan. Moving the cement blocks from the door, she pondered which direction to take, and resolved on north. This was directly away from civilization as they once knew it, as yet unexplored, and therefore potentially fruitful.

Cold it was, but good to be moving. She had torn some of the surviving cloth from a burnt pair of curtains and wrapped it round her hands to stave off the worst of the cold. Scrambling over the high ground the chill wind cut through her small frame like a hundred knives. She wondered if she should have left that blanket behind.

The landscape was almost bare. Small pockets of marsh grass struggled to hang on to existence; dead bracken and moss created an atmosphere of impressionist bleakness. The jaundiced colours were beautiful in their way, and outcrops of granite glistened their quartz grains in the milky sunshine. Far in the distance Barwin could see a thin trail of smoke. She estimated it to be a couple of miles away, and it could not go uninvestigated.

She dodged about, keen to stay out of sight. It made the journey longer, but she would only be seen when she chose to be.

The trail of smoke, her most reliable datum point, vanished after a while. Barwin guessed that it had been a night fire, and the occupiers didn't want to be found any more than she did. Taking her bearings from the clumps of trees she had mentally mapped, she worked her way to the place her mind had etched, tacking like a sailboat in the calm.

A small copse provided some shelter from the cutting wind and low temperature on the hills, and she crept in, sensing that she was not alone. It was highly unlikely that an animal of any size was around, yet with the general mayhem after the hurricane, many farm animals had found their way to freedom, some had survived. Pigs, cows and chickens in particular could be found in some very strange places. Being startled by a roosting chicken in a high-rise apartment was once fairly common. But most had been unceremoniously eaten. People didn't seem to realise that the chicken came before the egg, at least if you wanted to eat one.

Her senses had been right. As she carefully picked her way through the thicket of brambles, making a mental note that here was a place to come in the autumn for blackberries and acorns, she saw a lone figure crouching against a tree, male by the looks. He hadn't detected her. She took a closer look to see if he was armed. Nothing obvious, but probably a knife at least. His head was in his hands.

"Hello," she said from a distance, keeping her voice as low as was practicable under the circumstances. He didn't look up. In fact, he was so still he might have been dead. She threw a small stick at him. He looked up unconcerned. His face was mild, sorrowful, and his general demeanour was of complete dejection.

"Hello," she said again, a bit louder. He turned in her general direction. There was nothing about him which looked threatening, so she walked a little closer. "You OK?"

He tried a smile. "What's OK?"

"You know, not hurt or anything." she tried.

The smile became a little lopsided. "Nah. Just hungry."

She had to laugh "We're all hungry. It's the natural state."

He turned away almost crying. "I'm not used to it."

Deciding that he was highly unlikely to threaten her, she sat down beside him. He was strangely dressed – well, smartly dressed, which was strange enough in itself – if a little dishevelled.

He looked a bit older than her, possibly taller, on the skinny side. "How come you are here?"

It was fairly usual for random meetings to involve an exchange of practicalities. Survival was everything. Learning was essential.

He weighed her up suspiciously. "Ran out of food."

This was interesting. Nobody normal ran out of food because they usually didn't have any to run out of in the first place. Barwin had run out of food four years ago.

She opened the conversation with something about herself to break the ice. She told him how the city in which she once lived had quickly deteriorated into street violence after Angelo. How the infrastructure had crumbled and how she was forced to abandon her home, dragging her grandmother with her. She didn't know exactly where she was, but she knew that over the four years since they had been on the move, she had travelled about two hundred miles – not always in one direction. She told him her name, and asked for his.

He looked at her strangely, that lopsided grin flickered, but resorted to a grimace. "Sebastian," he said. "I don't know where I live, and I don't know where I am. I'm not really sure that I care anyway." This seemed to settle the matter from his perspective, and he looked back down in the general direction of his knees.

"So what happened to you?" Barwin tried.

There was silence, then a small, slightly unbalanced laugh. "The staff all left the house, and we had nothing to eat, and people were shooting at us, so I ran. I ran away, just anywhere." And his voice faded away into the middle distance along with his gaze. "I ran away. I couldn't help it…" and his shoulders shook in a pitiful despair.

To Barwin this specimen was about the least likely survivor she had ever come across. His dress, his attitude, his voice, everything about him shouted 'incapable'.

It was tempting to just move on and leave him in the depths of his own self-pity, but that was not Barwin's way. This man, she observed, though years older than herself, needed not so much a meal as a mother. The spectre of another dependent loomed.

She tried coaxing him into sharing more details, and although he was dizzy with tiredness and hunger, he seemed to be grateful for the diversion.

It transpired that Sebastian had been a stockbroker, a young high-flier with money to burn and a couple of expensive houses, cars and various other useless commodities rendered obsolete by civil unrest and food shortages. When order in the towns disintegrated, he moved with some staff to his country house which had several acres, and an old walled kitchen garden. They had been left unmolested by a quirk of geography – in that there were rivers on two sides, mountains behind, and no major roads. The eight inhabitants lived a reasonably good, if cloistered existence, until the harvest failed. Then they ate through their stores of food, and most of the remaining farm animals and game they could find. The staff, seeing the writing on the wall, started to steal anything which could be useful, then they took all the remaining food, the horses, and were gone.

A few days later a small gang of armed marauders had laid siege to the house, shots were fired, and Sebastian had escaped, more through luck than guile.

Barwin concluded that this man, though in her terms he was barely a man, was in shock. He had ridden out the intervening years of hardship for the many, by the cosseting cushion of wealth remaining to the few, but that was not enough, not on its own. He had no instinct for survival.

"Did the gangs get your food supplies, your seed? Did they take everything? What was left?

Sebastian looked at her hopelessly, that lop-sided grin flirted with the corners of his mouth. He laughed a sad, helpless laugh. "There wasn't anything left to take."

A Master of the Universe, living in the wrong universe. He might have cried tears, if there had been any left.

Barwin considered. A large country house, fortified to some extent, with access to water, which once had cattle, and probably hens, land, implements, maybe a copse… it would be worth exploring, later, when she could be sure the gangs had taken what they wanted and left.

"What was the house called?"

"Waldenby. On Hensford Moor," He muttered into the distance.

She made a mental note and changed the subject. "Did you see that trail of smoke over there?" waving in a north easterly direction.

He looked blank.

"OK," she said, realising that his powers of observation hadn't been enhanced since the literal fall of the stock market. "I'm off to explore it before it gets dark. Do you want to come?"

"Can't," he said. "Leg."

She crawled round to his other side, and could see the bloodstain on his torn suit trousers. A cursory look showed it to be a gunshot wound. Not dire, but in need of attention. She wondered that he hadn't fainted at the thought.

"You'll live," she announced upon a crude inspection. "Build yourself some shelter, and I'll come back."

"Yeah," he said, intimating that he didn't actually expect her to.

With that she meandered her way out of the copse with the intention of finding where the source of the earlier smoke came from.

The day was bleak. To keep from getting too cold, she ran a bit faster, keeping as low as she could among the bracken and stony outcrops. Boggy patches were unavoidable, and her boots let in water, but she pushed on. Days were short at this time of year, and she needed to be back on 'home' territory before twilight.

There was still no sign of a dwelling, and Barwin reluctantly decided it might just have been an open fire on the heath. She judged she would have about an hour before she should abandon the search.

Pausing at low tree, bent and deformed by the westerly winds, she sniffed the air. It held the unmistakable taint of cold ash; metallic, musty, dusty. She crouched and strained her ears. Nothing. She looked around for signs of trampled undergrowth. Nothing. Creeping forward a few yards, she saw some slabs of granite. It was intriguing. Her intuition told her someone would be there, but she needed a good look. No risks.

She crawled nearer, and felt rather than heard footsteps. She froze, belly to the ground. Ear to the ground. The unmistakable munching sound of foot on ground. She waited, not wanting to be trapped in this place, not wanting to be discovered.

Minutes ticked by and the sound retreated. She took out her knife. Crawling, dragging, unbreathing she inched forward to a gorse bush courageously pushing forth a single yellow flower bud. The spiny leaves scratched her face. A man was talking softly to himself, his back to her.

She inched herself carefully upwards through the spiky bush, and there it was, a carn, a pile of large stones forming a shelter, or maybe an ancient burial chamber. It was situated in a small depression in front of a good-sized rock. A mountain pool was nearby, fed by tiny streamlets. The ground around was clear of bracken and heather, as if at one time it had been cultivated. There looked to be enough room inside to shelter a handful of people, for a while anyway. Nothing lived up here, nothing much grew, or could be grown. If this man has a stash of food, she thought, he'd better hang on to it.

Slipping quietly down through the bush, Barwin retraced her steps. The cloud was forming low, and she needed to make haste, for the misty moors were as good as witchcraft to confuse the wanderer.

Stealth no longer paramount, Barwin ran fast over the rugged ground. Her sense of direction was good, and time was short. Reaching the fringe of woods where she had left Sebastian, she paused to catch her breath. Light was fading, but her senses were enhanced. She listened. It was the wrong kind of silence. Almost as if the worms had given up tunnelling.

She picked her way to the tree where she had last seen Sebastian. Gloom was all around. Straining her eyes, there was no sign of the crouched form she had expected to see. Yet there was something. A dark shape hung from the branches, a melancholy fruit, swaying gently, just above the spot.

Barwin suddenly felt exhausted. Her shoulders drooped, and a strong feeling of hopelessness overcame her. The long slim shape of Sebastian hung still before her eyes. His childlike face lolling to one side, a slightly baffled expression on his face, as if he had taken himself by surprise. Glistening dribble, not quite dry, ran from one side of his mouth, legs hanging limp, toes turning slightly in, like a hesitant child.

She knew she had to go through his pockets, take his clothing, shoes, anything and maybe everything, yet even their small conversation had invoked pity and compassion in her. Barwin wasn't hardened enough to raid dead people automatically. Here was a man, like so many others, who simply could not cope with the reality of living like a rat. For rat she was. Intelligent, wily, scavenging, exploitative. Living on the outside, darting here and there to grab supplies then vanishing again. There were no laws of either church or state to govern behaviour now, just the ongoing fear of contamination from plague victims, and the fear of starvation. There was life and death, and not much in between. In his simple wisdom, Sebastian had made his choice. No gamble here, the trading floors had not found favour with his stock. He cut his losses. Sold short.

She exhaled a long and resigned breath, climbed the tree, and cut him down. She removed her mind from the task in hand and stripped his body bare. There would be time later to go through the pockets. Quickly she formed a tidy bundle and, slinging it over her back, hastily ran in the direction of what could be called home. Burying the dead had long gone out of fashion.

Dog

Grandmother asked no questions when the next day they went through the bundle of belongings which was all that remained of Sebastian. It was a strange harvest. Apart from the clothing, which was of durable quality and instantly in use (though seeing her grandmother in a pin-striped jacket was a hard joke to overcome), there was a small paper photograph of a family group, an internet watch (useless, as there was no internet), a leather wallet with some money in it (equally useless as no one wanted money), a cotton handkerchief, suitably initialled with the family crest, a fountain pen, a bright yellow (possibly child's) hair slide, and a small bunch of keys.

"Every cloud has a silver lining," said Gran contentedly as she examined the fountain pen, which had no ink in it, which hardly mattered because there was no paper to write on anyway. Barwin wondered if her gran would ever run out of platitudes.

It was all potential bargaining power in a world stripped of almost everything worth bargaining for. Chief among them was probably the yellow hair slide. Barwin put it in her hair. It was quite pretty, with enamelled flowers of green and purple and blue. The colours of the suffragettes, who thought they had won everything with the vote, and found they had won nothing but a vote.

Sitting around was not in her nature, so doing a mental stock take of what they had in terms of food and other resources, Barwin decided she'd see what scratching around the nearby locality could reveal. A watery sun had pierced the gloom of the last few days. It was a good day for a mooch around.

Most of the detached houses near the road had been barricaded and fortified with whatever could be found. Old doors, barbed wire, farm fencing, public parks, public buildings, churches and mosques; if it could be carried it was up for grabs. No one cared who might own it, because no one actually owned anything they could not defend, and no one was defending the synagogues unless they lived in them. In every case where people had crowded together for safety, they had succumbed to the Mallavirus, the plague. Proximity to others was a death sentence. Live on the outside or die on the inside.

The silence around the houses was punctuated by the bark of a dog. Insistent, high-pitched barking.

Barwin had no idea how many, or indeed if any, of the houses were occupied. Gone were the days of friendly neighbours. People grasped and protected everything which remained to them. Behind barricaded doors the loneliness and savage trial of survival lived out its interminable days, weeks and years of waiting, waiting for something to turn up, to improve, to put things back the way they were. Except the way they were was the very thing which caused this catastrophe to happen. No, Barwin had it right. You survived, and you searched, and you planned.

She had a dream. A dream of an island. On this island a few people would be safe to coax the land back to life, to exist peacefully, and to rebuild a sense of order based on compassion and respect for all things living. An island big enough for animals and humans to thrive together, and above all, an island with enough food and heat for all. But she wasn't just a dreamer, she fully intended to make it happen. Every day of her life was orientated towards this goal. Every conversation, every clue, every speck of information, could be used to build a picture in her mind in readiness for the possibility of finding the right people, the right place, and the right time. The time was not now, she knew that, for the land was not ready yet, poisoned it would remain for a while to come. Maybe years. It didn't matter. She would be ready when the land was.

In the meantime there was the small matter of staying alive.

Barwin slunk round the outskirts of the houses. She wasn't looking for anything in particular, just opportunity. The gutters of the road were blocked with plastic detritus, some partly decomposed, some not. It was all useless, and had been picked over a hundred times before. She skirted the edge of the buildings where once a wood had been. Just tree stumps now, and some weakly sprigs of bramble. Everything had gone so quickly. People cut down trees for fires and didn't plant new ones, not that young trees stood much of a chance in the alternating bitter cold and searing heat. Someone might have made an effort, but tomorrow always came with hardships of an existential nature. Unfortunately tomorrow, in terms of ecology, was an unaffordable luxury.

This was indeed a barren landscape. Devoid of anything useful, not even a splinter of wood. She wound round the back of the houses and could hear that dog again. It was whining. The whole area seemed deserted, and in truth she was in need of a diversion, so she made for the place where the sound came from.

The backs of the houses were as well fortified as the fronts. Most people had run out of ammunition by now, so she was only slightly wary of being shot at. Nevertheless, normal precautions were required, so she soft-footed her way to the place where the sound was loudest, and tried her hand at moving the weakest point of garden enclosure. It was basically corrugated iron sheeting tied together with barbed wire. Holes had been drilled in the sheeting, and the wire threaded through. In this way a patchwork of bits and pieces had been carefully stitched together. Moving the sheeting made the usual sort of grating noise, so she rattled it a bit and crouched out of sight. No shouting, no movement. She rattled it again, harder, and the dog began to bark. Maybe it was alone.

Not having the means to cut the wire, Barwin crept round the perimeter. There was a lot of barbed wire. Eventually she came to a patch of old wooden fencing near the ground. She pulled at a piece of it, and it cracked. Three rotten pieces of wood removed, and there was room for her to wriggle through. The dog kept up a low grumble, but it did not approach her, even when she waggled her hand through the gap, so she warily pushed herself through.

The garden was quite nicely kept, with remnants of strawberry plants, their leaves brown from the winter frosts. The paths were swept and plant pots from a time when you could grow something useful in them, were stacked neatly in the corner. She stepped gingerly towards the house, and lying on the ground was a man, and the dog, tied to his arm. It didn't seem like a trap.

"You OK," she said enquiringly.

The dog, a skinny mongrel with random patches of brown and brindle, whined quietly.

"Helooo," she tried, wondering if the man was dead. He might have been, but was showing no signs of decomposition. She wondered if desperately hungry dogs ate their own humans in times of need.

The body let out a moaning grunt, a gritted plea of pain and desperation.

Barwin went closer.

"Can I help you?" she tried, then reeled back. There was a large pustule on the side of his forehead. It was Mallavirus. She knew the signs. And she now knew why these houses were deserted. There was no remedy but death for this ancient virus which had surfaced out of the melting tundra and forced its foul malevolence across a despairing world.

She didn't know if her body had developed immunity. She didn't know if the virus had mutated. For sure she had lived this long, and encountered the virus several times before. It was impossible to obliterate the sounds of suffering, the cries of help to one deaf deity or another, the panic as she had run with her father, his hand gripping hers so hard that she screamed in pain when they had accidentally come across a dumping ground for the nearly dead. It had got him, the virus, that is how she came to be marooned in a sea of calamity with only her fading grandmother to call a friend.

Barwin felt she should at least untie the dog from his arm. She was summoning the courage when the man muttered indistinctly, "There's food… take it… take him… take…" then curled his body and groaned that desperate groan which she knew only too well to be among his last. "Take…." He tried again, but never finished the sentence as the all-consuming cramps took hold of his disfigured body. His face contorted in agony. She looked away. She couldn't help him, no one could. He would know that.

Barwin, of course, was going to take whatever she could, though in a virus ridden house she knew it was risky. She tied her scarf around her face to try and put a barrier between his breath and hers. It at least hid her look of distaste as she pulled the dog's string free from his arm. Not that the dog was showing any signs of moving.

You die of hunger or you die of plague. Or both. She took her chances and entered the house. It had escaped the mob. Maybe this person had defended it well, or maybe the thought of plague had turned others away. A clock ticked. It was curious. Barwin hadn't any memory of hearing a clock tick. The clocks of her childhood had been powered by anything other than clockwork. Against the background of the sombre and precise ticking of the clock, she searched the house. It was scarcely believable that one single house, in all her experience, had remained intact. It was like a museum, but not of her time, of a time before. Maybe her grandmother's time. But time itself was ticking away, so she made haste to go through the kitchen cupboards. Biscuits. Tins. Rice. Bottles of wine. Brandy. Dried pulses. It was a treasure trove, and she stuffed her backpack with all it could carry and left yet more. She would return.

Inching her way past the dying man, Barwin thought about the dog. It looked at her, then lay down on its belly, resting its head on the arm of the afflicted man. Sentimentality, like law and order, was dead, yet she felt something. Pity maybe, or maybe something deeper. The dog did not move as she made her way back through the fence, nor did it make a sound, but its eyes followed her. She could feel them.

"Were the shops nice, dear?"

Gran was stirring from one of her extended sleeps. Possibly she had hoped to awake to her version of normality, possibly she had just blotted out reality.

"Not bad, Gran," Barwin replied, humouring her as she unpacked her rucksack. "Look, I've got you some wine and look, brandy as well. Shall we open a bottle?"

Gran looked very pleased. "Yes, why not. Go and get the glass decanter out of the cupboard and bring two wine glasses will you, dear – the ones with the pretty pink stems."

Obviously they didn't have any glasses, never mind a decanter. Barwin could see the funny side of it. If depression was the natural state of mind, it was what you did to overcome it which made living another day possible.

She chuckled. "Sorry, Gran, we're fresh out of glasses, you'll have to drink straight from the bottle." She unscrewed the wine bottle and handed it to her grandmother, who took it with gusto, laughingly confiding that this wasn't the first time she had drunk wine from a bottle, and recounted the day when she and her first husband went to the seaside for a picnic and no one packed the glasses.

"Much better to forget the glasses than the corkscrew, eh, love?" And she tipped her head back and demolished about a third of the bottle straight off. Barwin smiled. Hopefully a drunk and disorderly grandmother wouldn't be too much of a handful. As if in response, her grandmother twinkled her blue eyes and burst into life. She rose unsteadily to her feet and announced she would tidy the house, took another large glug of wine, and sat down again, less tidily, but impishly amused by everything in general.

It was better, she hoped, that her gran enjoyed her little tipple whilst she could. Feeling emboldened, Barwin downed a mouthful of brandy to keep her company. It was disgusting.

Alcohol aside, they would dine well tonight. Lots of lovely tins of things unheard of came out of the rucksack, and Barwin was in the mood for experimentation. She first needed to see if it was safe to light a fire. If it was, they would eat themselves full, because tomorrow it would be time to think about moving on.

Ben

It was not a sure thing that having escaped the virus thus far, she would always escape it. But that store of food was much too good to leave open to all comers, not that there were any comers, not now at least. This forgotten corner of pestilence, long abandoned, steeped in the stillness of death passing over, and over, was bequeathed to her alone. If even accident could aid her existence, it was unhappy accident, overcome by the forceful power of youth and ignorance. Some would live, some would die. By whose hand it was unclear. Darwin had his place in the stifling rooms of scientific observance, his monkey men making monkey men of them all. Luck or judgement, both had their theories hammered out in Victorian parlours. No Victorian had envisaged a million-year-old virus hatching out of the frozen tundra and taking an evolutionary leap across the echoes of time itself. Divine judgement met prodigious luck in nature's experimental wastelands.

She felt compelled to check if the dog had left the house, or whether it had decided to die by its owner. Canine luck, canine judgement or canine choice. It might have had the choice, it might have had the luck, it might even have the judgement. Poor moth-eaten scrap, freed from the tenuous bond of a piece of string it might have gnawed through days ago, lying in the waiting room of divine interference, would have to make its own choice.

Something in the way it had looked at her had forged a tenuous connection. Maybe it was the eyes, or that one bent ear, or that calm steady look, imparting feelings not words, an alien language, but with links discernible as long as you didn't rationalize them. Barwin had never kept an animal of any kind, had no particular feelings for them, and was not the rescuing sort, but she felt an interest in this moth-eaten hound.

Where to store the food was an altogether more challenging concern. If the Mallavirus still lingered in these parts, she should be leaving them quickly. It had crossed her mind that she should go and see the man living in the stone-slabbed carn. Intuition maybe, but an extra pair of hands would be good, and if he was indeed on his own, maybe she could trade something with him.

The weather held dry, she knew where she was going, her grandmother was sleeping off the bottle of wine, and the dog could wait for her return. Sliding watchfully out of the house, she dipped and cantered in the general direction of the carn. Never in a straight line, always on guard. She avoided the small copse where the remains of Sebastian might still be visible (though surely there were enough hungry animals to make short of his skinny form) and swung round to the right which would take her on an as yet unexplored route. Here were no paths, no tracks, just the faded greyish bracken and scrubby grass poking up between the granite giants. A couple of hours later, when she felt she was near, she slowed her pace, until creeping closer she could just make out the line of stone slabs peering above the rugged horizon.

She poked her trailing hair back into her cap and pulled her scarf up to her ears. She needed to look boyish. As she crept closer she could see no sign of the man. The place felt empty, so, knife in hand, she said 'hello' inquiringly. Unsure where the entrance to this cave-like abode actually was, she skirted round it, and tried 'hello' again. Nothing. This was disappointing.

Of course she had to look inside. Finding a reasonable gap between the stones, she eased her way slowly in. Nothing much was evident in the way of comforts. No bed, no seating, just bundles of wood tied together with some kind of twine. Scraps of animal skin hung up on a line, a cooking pot and a battered enamel mug. She squatted down on her haunches, surveyed some marks drawn in the dry earth, and resolved to wait for a while in case the occupier returned.

She would wait outside.

Not for her the surprise element of him coming in and trapping her in this confined place. She'd been trapped before, and raped. Why did men have to do this to women? Was it simply a power trip? Or just male inadequacy made visible? It felt to her that rape was just another form of intimidation employed by some men to keep insecure women in a state of fear. Well, she'd been raped and she wasn't scared of them or their pathetic attempt at psychological dominance.

She remembered the cold stare of the man who had cornered her, punched her, violated her. As he forced his way into her, she felt an overwhelming sense of loathing. There was no fear, because she fully expected him to kill her afterwards, but it was vile. He was vile. Slathering, grimacing, pummelling at her barely formed breasts, drowning her in his stinking breath, globs of spittle dripping on her face and that disgusting penis shoving itself between her unwilling legs. The rape itself had been painful, but not as painful as the recurring thought that it could happen again. She knew she would kill the next man to rape her. In a way she was always ready to. It was her recurring demon, the dark thought that haunted the recesses of her restless mind. It was as if she wanted to be close to rape again so that she could take her vengeance out on the next man and atone for her girlish lack of courage in one instance, with the blood of another.

Satisfied that she was in a fairly safe position, she settled down watchfully, fascinated by two black ants which scuttled across her boot. She liked insects, for there was so few of them, and it was a forgotten privilege to see them at work, here in the wilderness where little seemed to survive, if it survived anywhere.

"Hey!" came a voice from she knew not where. Surprised, she glanced quickly around. There was no body to accompany the voice.

"Here!" The voice came from the carn, which surprised her, as she had not seen anyone enter it. As she had come with the specific intention of meeting this person, she decided to be polite, if cautious.

"Hello," she replied, "I thought you were out."

He smiled. It was a modest smile, working its way out from under some peculiarly overlarge spectacles. "Not out."

To avoid a conversation of ludicrous suburban niceties, Barwin got straight to the point. She asked if he was on his own, asked if he needed supplies, asked how he was surviving.

To this last question he laughed. "Surviving? I'm surviving, though I'm not sure why." His voice was light, friendly.

She laughed back. None of them knew why they were surviving. Things hadn't got better in years. Depopulation had been the only useful outcome, less mouths to feed.

They conversed at a safe distance of about five metres. He was unarmed, she brandished a knife. She told him she had access to a store of food and drink which was too much for her to carry or store. In return she would require shelter for probably some weeks.

He settled his languid frame onto a smooth-topped stone, and weighed up the bargain. In truth, he could do with some company, having lived alone for more than a year. If that company came with its own supplies, so much the better. He said he'd come with her if she put the knife away. She said she wouldn't. He pulled on a coat and came anyway. The days were too short to be dithering around building trust. Everything was instinctive. He thought he could probably trust her. She thought she could probably trust him. That was as good a bargain as any.

Barwin didn't mention her grandmother. Discretion at this point was the better part of valour. She didn't mention the plague either.

They walked together, talked a little about their recent past. Both were watchful – of each other as well as the wider environment. Both had survived thus far, with reason. She deduced that he was about fifty years old, and his previous life as a woodsman had prepared him well for the disasters which had changed everything. He could hunt, he could live off the land quite adequately. Although a person of few words, he seemed to be polite and courteous. For his part, he perceived Barwin as a gutsy little survivor who would be refreshing company, even if she might stab him in the night.

What Barwin didn't know, was that this man had carved out a comfortable subterranean area under the carn, having decided that this was as good a spot as any to throw down a tenuous root. Sheltered from the prevailing wind, masked by the lay of the land, the arrangement of natural features had once been chosen as a spiritual place to rest the ancestors. A holy place. Untouched for millennia. Guarded only by the old gods, the ones that made sense. Gods of sun and rain and harvest. Gods of life. Newer gods had seeded the apocalypse. War and shame their only legacy. He was happy enough with the thought of the old gods for company.

Erring on the side of caution, Barwin took a circuitous route to the group of houses where the food supplies were. The area was deathly quiet, and there was every chance the house would be untouched since her visit the day before. When they were just metres away, she mentioned the plague. He shrugged. He had seen it all before.

The dog whined quietly as they shimmied through the gap in the fence. Poor thing, it looked to be going the way of its owner, but it got up and made a valiant attempt to greet Barwin, then sat again exhausted. The man was dead. The smell was abhorrent. They quickly packed all they could into makeshift bags, coats, rucksacks and, bizarrely, suitcases found in an upstairs room. Barwin eyed a quilted bedcover longingly. Her companion found some tools in a shed.

They carried what they could to the house where Barwin and her grandmother stayed, and walked in.

"This is my grandmother," said Barwin casually, knowing this would go down like a lead balloon. The man chuckled. There had to be a catch.

Grandmother, upon seeing the stranger, fiddled uselessly with her hair as if she had some sort of hairstyle worth fiddling with, and gave a girlish smile. "I didn't know you were bringing a friend to tea, dear. Better sit down whilst I put the kettle on." There was obviously no kettle, nor for that matter was there anything to sit on. There certainly wasn't any tea. Grandmother made to get up, but the clink of empty bottles explained very nicely why she could not. The brandy bottle was empty.

'Oh dear,' thought Barwin, 'a drunken deranged old lady was not going to be helpful.' She shrugged nonchalantly, and explained that the trophy alcohol from the day before was not a usual habit. In truth she had no idea how her grandmother was going to get to the carn, but, as ever, that was a bridge which would be crossed in the fullness of time. It had taken days to get Gran to this place. It would probably take days more to get her anywhere else.

"I'd like to introduce you, but I don't know your name," said Barwin to her new companion.

"You didn't ask."

Barwin looked at him in exasperation. "OK, I'm asking now."

"Ben. And you, my friend, are the barbarian of myth and fable." He was mocking her, just slightly.

She put him right with a cold stare.

A faint scratching noise came from the door they had just entered the house by. Barwin already knew what it was likely to be. She opened the door, and the sad-faced dog slowly walked into the house. It was inevitable. She knew from the moment she saw him that there would be an attachment. Ben greeted him comfortingly, and he was given some food left from the feast of the night before, which was suitably demolished.

It was a strange little group which sat by the feeble fire that night. The dog, Gran, Ben and Barwin.

None of them had much to say, they all knew the stories, the tales too difficult to tell, the scenes best forgotten. There was only the now, and silent thoughts of how they would manage tomorrow, and the relative peace only a morbidly silent night could bring. Each in their own thoughts, deafened by the sound of words unsaid, contemplating the ruddy embers of recalcitrant heat, they sporadically spoke of practicalities, and planned a move which would take place over a period of days.

To the Carn

The matter of logistics decided, they rose early to be rid of these plague-ridden houses. "Where there's a will there's a way," announced grandmother in one of her never-ending series of platitudes. There did at least seem to be the will.

Ben and Barwin would make a start by carrying everything they could to an approximate halfway point. Barwin would then go back and collect Gran, Ben would collect more supplies. If Gran could make it halfway before sundown, Barwin would spend the night in the open with her, whilst Ben continued ferrying supplies from the house to the carn. It was a plan bound to fail.

In the event, Gran couldn't make more than a quarter of the journey in one go. Her legs just didn't seem to want to walk any more despite her insistent "Mind over matter" mumblings along the way. Her spirit was reasonably willing, but really she wanted an end to all this horrible existence. She kept going because she didn't want to leave her granddaughter all alone in this unfathomably inhospitable world. It was hard for the old to adjust. They had had it so good.

The old lady had to be left wrapped in all manner of abandoned bits of clothing and covers for the night whilst the urgent business of transferring provisions carried on around her. The weather turned warmer, and wetter. That Gran survived at all was testament to her iron constitution – something her granddaughter was glad to inherit.

Three days later they were all finally installed in the carn. Dog came with them, nose umbilically attached to Barwin's heel. So far they had all escaped symptoms of the plague virus. Gran was surprisingly chipper, for a woman who slept most of the day. "All in a day's work," she beamed as she staggered inside the welcoming shelter of the carn. Gran seemed to have fallen back on platitudes as her sole means of communication.

Those who were awake surveyed the magnificent larder stacked up in the underground space. It had been worth the effort. The rest of this year was taken care of for the three of them – and Dog – if they were careful.

Going North

The winter expended its dreary darkness of mist and bog and wetness, and a hot dry spring followed quickly on its heels. Barwin adjusted from scavenger to predator, much against her usual instincts. She learnt to hunt the diminishing wildlife, and learnt too that the very act of hunting them was part of their diminution. Spring was too hot. Too dry. The fledgling green of new grass abandoned hope and withered before seed could set. The tired brown of winter gave way to the lamenting brown of drought. Only the granite stones stood unapologetic, casting ever shorter shadows, mocking the fragile struggle for life beneath them.

Scouting the few miles around them brought increasing concern, for the countryside was more barren than the town. The silent wait for rabbit or hare became futile. Gran had happily said, "The thing about rabbits is that they breed like rabbits," in expectation of fresh meat to come. She was wrong. If there was any breeding, it was not here.

Reproduction discontinued, abandoned, postponed until further notice.

Nothing moved bar the callous dry wind. It was like being in the waiting room of the extinction of all things. All things great and small, wise and wonderful, the great creation in reverse. Once they saw a bird, a crow maybe, they followed its soaring path for hours until it disappeared over the northern horizon. Dog, healthier now, couldn't even find an imaginary scent to follow. A great emptiness yawned across the moors where there had once been ponies, skylarks, beetles and gnats. Life existed in only one sad little gorse bush, three persevering humans and a faithful dog.

Barwin and Ben had struck up an odd friendship. She just fifteen (approximately) and he forty-five (he thought), they became a team, constantly on the lookout, looking out for each other. Similar in outlook, both prone to waiting and weighing, both practical, neither prone to words, they easily learned to read each other in movement and thought. There was nothing remotely sexual about their relationship; indeed there was no common attraction. Their friendship was a means to an end. Maybe, just maybe, if they turned out to be the last people to walk the earth, they would do something about procreation, but it was never discussed. In any case, until they found a properly sustainable way of living, there was no point even thinking about it. He respected her. She respected him. That was all there was to it.

Gran was becoming less chatty as she became less wakeful. Still relatively healthy, though almost burrow-ridden as she seldom left the standing stones of the carn, she could still summon a platitude at the drop of a hat. It was all the entertainment they got, expending ever more calories in the decreasing hope of finding a decent source of calories was no fun, but they developed a kind of black humour to tide them through the tough times. A gritty humour. Laughing about what they'd put on their tombstones.

"Told you I was hungry," was a favourite of Ben's.

"Red hair doesn't die, it doesn't even fade away," was Barwin's current favourite.

They taught each other songs, harmonised, made up the words which they didn't know and tried to imitate remembered wildlife sounds. In the whole spring they didn't see a fox, or a bird. Just that solitary crow. The silence was almost unbearable.

But as day followed day, Barwin would come out of the carn and look at the gorse bush – the same one she had hidden in months before, and admire its tenacity for survival. A yellow flower here, a couple more there. Always a flower. Laughing at the odds. Always a sign to her that life is possible under any circumstances. It became her private emblem. She too was laughing at the odds, and she didn't even know what they were.

"When gorse is out of flower, kissing's out of season," Gran would remark every other day – each time as if it was the first time – and glancing a visual nudge at Barwin or Ben as if they might just get the hint, which was unlikely. They were hunting partners, fellow survivors with deep respect for one another, and respect deeper still for the harsh environment in which they had been plunged. Gran's coquettish ways could have been irritating to these two independents, but instead her squeamish attempts at matchmaking were greeted with quiet humour, and maybe a wink, now and then. It was the nearest they got to cabaret.

"North it is," said Barwin finally after the discussion which summed up their situation. "Gran, you know you'll have to stay here, and you know I'll come back when we find something better." Her grandmother seemed not to care much either way. There was no promise of a party, either way.

Neither of them had been north. South, east and west were roughly known, and discounted. South was the lowlands and the cities where they expected the Mallavirus to be still running its devious course. Visions of rotting bodies and desperate gangs still haunted Barwin. West and east had been mapped out by Ben over the years: These were the intermediate lands where more resourceful survivors like himself had opted for relative freedom and marginal survival. North might be cooler, might be wetter. The sea lay that way, with its dangers and unpredictability. It was time to try. Options decreasing.

Carrying what they could, they set off in a tolerable south-westerly wind. Goodbyes to Gran were swift. She had plenty of necessities and promised to guard them with her life. Dog glued to Barwin's heels, course set for the mountains, nothing to lose.

Higher they tramped, the wind speeding through their tattered clothes, boots fit for nothing cracked into broken stones. It was only hope which kept them going, the silly old hope that they never admitted to themselves or each other. The ridiculous hope that just over the next mountain there would be laid out before them a Garden of Eden full of fresh green grass, trees laden with fruit, birds and animals, rainbows and rivers. They knew it was ridiculous, but what is life without hope.

At the top of the first incline, Ben paused and looked back over the jagged curves of the moor they had just traversed. "Remember this, Bar, remember every bit of this view. It will be your way back."

The first night spent high in the sheltered crevices was bracing, the second night freezing, the third as good as death. They cleared the first high point, shaking with the cold, eager to see what lay beyond, but still there was more to climb, and high in the jet stream they shivered and strode, grateful for the company to cajole their flagging spirits, guarding their secret hopes close, but dreading the next reality.

They skirted the most jagged peaks, started the long downhill, but the moors seemed to carry on forever. Suddenly the land plunged away from them without warning. An abrupt revelation. Unprepared eyes. Stupefaction. A steep-sided valley spread green below, and it was a vision of everything they had never seen. U-shaped and deep, it was the result of a million years of icy invasion, a massive glacier lumbering infinitesimally slowly down the mountainside, grinding the rock away on either side, scouring the bottom of the valley smooth, and all that was left was a meandering stream snaking through fertile meadows. They laughed stupidly. Balmy and forgiving, it called them. With every step the valley became bigger, greener, more beautiful, more magical. It was another world, a shared dream, an electric impulse of something near pain which drove through the body as the brain sought to process what barely believing eyes could see. And the pain became more intense as they worried that this could not be, that the vision would dissipate before they had chance to touch it.

Something moved. Ben saw it first and put out his arm out to stop Barwin in her tracks. They dropped to the ground. Far below was a blackish speck, moving, then another, moving very slowly. Cattle, they guessed. Most probably someone had settled this place before them. Friend or foe. They would have to wait and see.

The terrible realization that they could not just go there, bathe in the stream, roll in the green, caught even Ben by surprise. Of course they could not just go there, not yet anyway. The visceral surge of longing had obliterated their senses. How could they be the first, how could they just walk into this heavenly place unmolested. They would have to be patient, and wait, and watch.

From higher still something was watching them. A bird. Maybe a crow. Maybe the same crow they had seen before. It wheeled overhead, circled above them, then went.

They struck yet another rudimentary camp. It was the sixth day since leaving the carn, and would be the sixth night in the open.

Far below, the two blackish specks merged with others and the group made their way slowly towards a small cluster of trees. Evening came, and the watchful pair perceived a wisp of smoke coming from those same trees. Humans.

Watch and wait.

They ate their last tins of unlabelled food. Chickpeas and mushrooms as it turned out, wiped them dry and stored them in the rucksacks. Everything was a resource for the future. There was no such thing as waste. A rag, a tin, a screw, a broken jar, everything was a resource, and even if there was no immediate use for it, there would be a use, one day. Gran had told them of the time when all such things were ritualistically thrown away every week – even beds and paper and entire fitted kitchens. Barwin had happened upon a huge rubbish dump some years ago. It was crammed with all manner of useful stuff. You could build a house and furnish it with what a previous generation had discarded.

Consumerism they called it. A throw-away society based on the terminally erroneous assumption that there would always be plenty of everything. She had scavenged what she could carry, but the rubbish dump was a dangerous place, guarded jealously by malicious people hanging on to the old ways. People who still thought ownership was power, before the food ran out. You could get shot for trespassing onto certain parts of the dump. You could get bullets, then.

They waited, and watched. Dog did not. He had caught the scent of something and could not contain himself. Scampering wildly across the rocks, he quickly plunged out of sight in a state of high excitement. It was pointless to stop him. He was a dog after all. It may be that he would be seen by those below, but that didn't have to matter. One manic dog thrashing about the hillside did not have to look like a threat.

When he returned he looked so unbelievably happy that you had to forgive him everything. It didn't look as though he had caught anything. He was just experiencing the simple joy of finding a new scent. He lay down on the rocks exhausted. His tail didn't stop wagging for hours.

The next day it appeared to be business as usual on the valley floor. The early mist burned back in gentle cloudy wisps, wafting up the sides of the valley until they evaporated without trace. The dark specks moved out of the trees and scattered laboriously. They could well be cows. Ben scouted the terrain thoughtfully, looking for viable paths, possible escape routes. His lean frame bending this way and that as he ducked behind rocks to conceal himself. Although they were still on relatively high ground, their vantage point was sheltered from the wind, and the early sun warmed them. The valley below teased their spirits with verdant greens and pastoral invitations. A microclimate of its own, they guessed, sheltered on every side but the far west, where the cliffs decreased in size and the entrance widened to the sunset.

"Can't be many people living there," offered Ben on his first return. All I've seen is a handful of animals.

"Animals," mused Barwin. "Life, beautiful life."

"Let's just make sure we hang on to ours, Bar."

She nodded. Not that she considered her life particularly valuable. It was life itself which caused the value. Life hung desperately to life, sometimes at any cost. Except for Sebastian. His was the only suicide she had witnessed, and she was still cross with him. The innate will to survive had forced her to be ingenious, resourceful and strong. She did not understand 'giving up'. Neither did she properly understand the circumstances which led to 'giving up'. She decided that Sebastian had thought that wealth and luxury could weather the crisis, and when they had disappeared, there appeared to be nothing left. Adapt or die, it seemed. The brutality of evolution.

There had been nine billion people living on the planet before the disasters. Far too many, said her mother, who had studied population and resource management. Those who had not died through virus, hurricane or malnutrition would have by now adapted. But one adaptation has to be followed by another when events move quickly, such as now. The day of the scavenger is surely over when there is nothing left to scavenge. Barwin had entered that new day when she found Ben. There was now the land and only the land, and for that land to yield life it too needed to adapt. Climate change had changed everything. The hurricane, the Mallavirus, would do their worst, but climate change was the bitter blow. The deathly blow of starvation visited bird and animal alike as the seasons moved haphazardly away from the norm. Too much dry in the time of growth, too much wet in the time of rest. Many trees had given up the fight, their carcasses strewn like jagged gravestones across the landscape. Occasionally there was evidence of one last struggle for survival, nervous bunches of leaves poking out from gnarled brown branches, trying for one last time to find favour with the elements, and failing, scorched where they were, not even chance to drop, decently, to the ground. The blasting heat of spring signalled no renewal, and wildlife across the globe felt the grinch of death as their food supplies faltered, then withered, then died. Adaptation was fine if there was something to adapt to.

Ben and Barwin knew they would have to go down to the valley on the third day. Their watchful eyes had seen no change in the routine below. Animals had come out from the trees in the morning, and gone back in the evening. The wisp of smoke appeared every night as the sun left the valley.

They tidied what little they had under a group of stones and, having agreed to go down empty-handed, they picked a way slowly down the steep-sided cliffs. The crow circled overhead.

Knowing they would be seen was part of the plan.

The Valley

The wind dropped to almost nothing as they made their descent. Small tufts of grass and lichen clung to the weathered rock. The going was steep; it required thought, for a dead end to a precipice would cost them dear in time spent retracing their steps. The tufts of grass gave way to small bushes, then stubby trees, and it got warmer, and despite the concentration employed to make a safe descent, they had a feeling of being followed.

Three hours of slipping and scraping along the knobbled crevices of limestone rock brought them to the bottom, and it was hot. The sun, merciless, reflected off the white cliffs, but their feet were buried in deepest green, greener than they imagined, greener still than any green they could remember. It was enough to just be there, in the moment, eyes caressing the wondrous joy of green.

The crow flew in through the trees, and they followed its path. A stone cottage lay hidden in the shade of spindly pines.

At the entrance of the cottage a new vision arrested their eyes. She held her arms out, palms facing towards them, the breeze wafted at her long grey hair and her dress worn thin as air clung round her legs and body. The crow alighted on her shoulder, and dipped its head. Together they fluttered in the dappled shade, woman and bird floating calmly in the breeze, a mysterious poem to nature's tranquillity.

Her eyes spoke of peace, and power. Her weathered face tilted slightly upwards to the sun as if in worship. A shiver ran down Barwin's spine. The woman was old, beautiful, serene. In that moment she owned the world.

"You have been expected." She smiled, deep wrinkles expressing themselves around her cool grey eyes. She motioned them in, silver bangles jingling prettily along her sinuous arms.

"Come, come and eat with us."

A small movement from behind announced the presence of another. A boy carrying a wooden spear stepped towards them. He looked ready to use that spear, mean and business-like for all his nine years of life. The boy moved quietly round them and joined the woman. It was a scene of gentleness and might.

The woman, strong-featured, slim to the point of bony, her authority over her domain palpable. The boy, her protector, trying to judge the newcomers, not yet ready to trust. The crow, between them, black and beady, shifting from foot to foot.

Barwin tried a greeting, apologising for being empty-handed, Ben bowed in awe. He had never seen such a woman. In her he saw the rivers and the sea, the sky and the earth. In her he saw his life, anew, and there were no words but the jarring of emotion, awakened by the seed of her very being.

Minas was her name. She passed them each a cup of sweet liquid, then sat and watched them drink. "It's good that you came now. The barometer is dropping fast, and the cliffs are no place for a stranger." And seeing their confused faces as they sipped the liquid. "Yes, it's honey. The dear bees have kindly agreed to stay with us."

Then she brought food. Small baked biscuits which were delicate to the mouth, filling to the stomach. "We get by here," she said, "and strangers are rare. It was good of you to give us time to prepare for your arrival." And all the time the crow stared down from her angular shoulder, weighing them suspiciously.

She motioned to the boy that it was time to fetch the animals. Plummeting air pressure meant storms of any velocity, or any duration. Ben and Barwin were anxious to help. Dog did some rudimentary herding of elderly cows which didn't need herding, for the change in air pressure was keenly felt by all life, and they were already making their way to shelter. Together they lifted rocks around the beehive to protect it, and a few tardy residents buzzed speedily home for safety.

Restless cows were corralled behind the cottage, shutters nailed down, everything which moved, or could be moved, was brought into safety, and then it started.

Howling from the west, the open end of the valley, came a monstrous wind. It roared and gathered itself in mountainous surges of salty spume. Lashing against the little cottage, crashing against the valley cliffs it came, gathering speed all the time. Gathering things, maybe trees, maybe animals, houses, maybe the entire detritus of humanity, and lashing its demonic whip in volley after volley of thundering punishment, and still there was more.

The cattle screamed.

Anxious eyes looked round the little space in the cottage. This felt like a big one, like Angelo. Minas lit a tiny beeswax candle. Hurricane Angelo had been four years ago. Barwin considered that just as they had found somewhere hopeful to stay, it was being ripped away from them. No good dwelling on what might be. Better to talk.

And so they delivered their stories in true folkloric fashion. Maybe a little embellished here, maybe a little left out there. Huddled round the tiny candle, they leaned in to catch the speaker's intonation. Minas and Ben sat close together, the skin on his forearm touching the skin on hers. You could feel the magic pulsating between them. You could feel the pain and the ecstasy as the electric fields surrounding them fought, spiked and merged. The invisible field twinkled in solace as each drew succour from the other, conjoining their very essence, and yet they didn't move, or even look at each other. It was as if two had become one.

Minas

Minas told her story first. She had cruised through life following only her spirit, and after various pointless jobs became an aid worker, which ultimately took her to Africa. Her instinct to alleviate the suffering became compromised after realising that famine and water shortage were impossible to stop. The over-heating of an already hot country could not be contained, even with all the technology and agricultural know-how on the planet. The only thing even remotely likely to arrest disaster was if the entire world stopped burning fossil fuels immediately. She finally judged the situation too difficult to bear. Waterhole after waterhole was sunk until there was barely any water left. Billions of gallons of bottled water were imported, plastic adding to the funeral pyre of humanity, money was raised, food sent, and it was all futile.

The deadly virus of Ebola, which had dithered about in central Africa since the 1970s pushed hardship onto hardship. The people of Africa were locked down and unable to travel. Aid workers were sent home, some of whom died under the most advanced medical treatment available. The death toll, once under control, started to rise again. Ebola was not leaving Africa, why should it. Governments in developed nations were only interested in keeping the virus away from their shores, not in eradicating it from Africa.

The central belt of Africa was now untenable. Minas came home and campaigned against the burning. She did everything she could to get the government to stop adding carbon to the atmosphere, but governments were intransigent. The big money did not even have to put up a fight. They had bought the battle decades before. Maybe it was too late anyway, but when people were brutally killed at a massive demonstration in the capital, her campaigning days ended. It was as pointless as throwing bottles of water at Africa. Too little too late.

Yet if the desert was destroying the fertility of Africa, the sea was destroying home. Her house was in a shallow sandy bay, set back from the sea, but the sea did not see that as an obstacle. Little by little it crept through the town, a few houses here, a few houses there, lost, waterlogged, and the people moved back up the hill. Some were caught up in storms and never seen again. Some just rebuilt elsewhere. It was a lazy pattern, and that was perhaps the problem.

Everyone had the information. Small incidents were absorbed, flash floods, sea swells, short periods of drought, and for the most part people dealt with them, and because they dealt with the smaller things, they thought they could deal with everything. Storms came and went. Heat came and went, flooding came and went, and in their self-congratulatory mood they did not prepare for the tragically foreseeable hurricane of hurricanes. No date had been set of course, but the scientists knew that the really big storms were as inevitable as the disappearing polar ice and the frying tropics stripped of their rainforests. It was an emotional problem. Something too big to contemplate, apocalyptic, beyond their ken. Rational, logical thought and reasoned discourse were trampled under the clamour for short-term gain. No one wanted to devalue the price of their house by admitting it was vulnerable, no one with any sense would buy it anyway. The time to cut your losses and rebuild life in a safer place came and went. People were still buying petrol cars, heating their houses with gas, and stocking up their larders with imported produce. It became a farce.

When the massive storms eventually did come, all the work of the scientists was rendered useless. Everyone could have planned decades before, but they did not. A human failing. Plan for tomorrow's lunch, but not tomorrow's epic disaster. Angelo was inevitable.

There was no hope that climate change could be reversed. The carbon in the atmosphere had steadily increased. The scientists said that three hundred and fifty parts of carbon per million was the limit of safety. It crashed through four hundred parts per million in the 1990s. It was in the news, yet only blind eyes saw it. Humanity sent their children to live on an unfamiliar planet of suffering undefinable. But the opposite of hope is not despair. It is grief. Even while resolving to limit the damage, many were already mourning. And the sheer scale of the problem provided a perverse comfort, for everyone was in it together. The swiftness of the change, its scale and inevitability, bound all together as one savagely broken heart, trapped under a warming atmosphere which would inevitably release dark secrets from the slumbering ice at the poles.

Minas abandoned her little house down by the sea and struck out for something, somewhere, which just might be safe. She studied the maps, travelled light, tried a few places, abandoned them, and eventually walked into this valley. From the map it didn't look particularly promising, just another valley, but as she followed the stream, camped by its pools, and ate from the hedgerows, she could see great potential in the ever-steepening sides. At the head of the valley it was almost a canyon, sheltered in every way but from the troublesome west. Of course, she wasn't the first to find it. There was a man. He took her in and together they farmed just enough to sustain themselves. He was kind and he was strong. Reclusive to a fault he may have been, but he asked her to stay. Eventually they made the boy (and she looked across the tremulous little gathering at him, as only a benign mother can) which she added was bit of a miracle as she was not so young in years.

Angelo had of course set them back. They lost their chickens, they lost their bull, they lost some sheep and cows, but the salty rage of the hurricane eventually subsided, and the land came fresh again as the little stream spread its cool clean water, percolated for years through layers of sedimentary rock, and fertility resumed. The man had left to find what he could to augment their herds, for the cows were getting old. He never came back. She and the boy had been without him for two years.

Minas's smile was enchanting. Ben had been telling the story of his simple life in the forestry, and every time she turned that radiant smile on him, he went a little bashful. He was not prone to speaking at length about anything, but the company insisted. It transpired that the female gender had not featured greatly in his life. An early girlfriend had baulked at the idea of living in a remote cabin, and wasted no time in settling down in suburbia with someone else. Infrequent trips to the nearest town resulted in nothing more than a few drinks with old friends. He eventually gave up the idea of finding a partner who would share his love of the beautiful outdoors. In his view, women seemed to be preoccupied with choosing material for their curtains, or lipsticks, or their job. The women who would have suited his temperament never crossed his path. Not once did he come across the female tree surgeon, the farmer or the carpenter. Towns and cities had sucked so many people into their orbit, often reluctant people just trying to earn a living, and he deliberately avoided the bright lights of excess. A loner he would remain. Not unhappy at all, for the countryside was his passion and his joy.

Climate change had lived with him from the beginning. He would walk the woodlands desperately listening out for his favourite birds as their numbers shrivelled. Year on year, evening after evening he would strain to hear the nightingale and the woodcock, the wagtail and the mistle thrush. Patchwork fields gave way to vast monocultures, cows were incarcerated in barns and could no longer be seen in fields, and the haunting sound of the curlew drifted into a forsaken past. He cursed the vile monoculture which accompanied pesticides and herbicides. He cursed the loss of the meadows, the demise of the bees, and his woods became almost silent, the dawn cacophony visiting only his dreams.

Ben had infinite, almost gullible faith in the goodness of the individual. But none whatsoever in the collective. He had lived in a world of many tiny acts of kindness, and it was the cruellest of realities that that world, as collective was incapable of stopping something so eminently stoppable as climate change. California burned. Islands and coastlines were smashed to oblivion by hurricanes. At night the stars were washed away by city lights, and human life was illuminated by the flickering ugliness of reality television. Decades beyond the point that it was known to be of the utmost stupidity, the urban dwellers continued to burn coal and oil and gas, heedless of the consequences.

He had lived it every day, far from the towns and cities, their noise and pollution, the changes bit into him like daggers. Death by a thousand knives, little by little, killing his world of the right to life. The Mallavirus had passed him by, the hurricane destroyed his house but that was no bother, he could build another, but he chose not to, wandering instead for something, anything. He met another wanderer, a delinquent lad spat out by the town, and they fell into step. The younger man was eager to learn how to survive, and Ben could show him the rudiments. But food on the land was diminishing as fast as it was in the cities, and they parted company. Soon after that Ben came across the carn, judged it safe enough, and set about creating a modest homestead. This was where Barwin found him.

Every storm could be the end. They drank a little more of the sweet honey and thyme liquor, and settled down for the long night, each comfortingly close to their neighbour. The psychotic cacophony of noise became deafening.

Barwin looked at the boy, who looked away, embarrassed. He had been afraid to look at her since they first met. She liked the way he looked: sturdy, tanned, long dark hair framing a face which was already showing signs of strong features. Probably he took after his father, because she could see very little sign of his mother's delicate features in him. For his part, the boy was fascinated by her thick mat of bright red hair, and her beautiful freckles, neither of which he had dreamed were possible in a human being. He stole surreptitious glances at her when he thought she wasn't looking. She, of course, was sensitive to this, and in the close proximity of the situation found it a little uncomfortable. He was a child who wasn't a child. His label of ten years seemed to announce him young, whereas her fifteen years announced her old. Five more years of interminable hardship had been endured, snatching what she could, running from the plague, from town to country and back again, experiencing death in epic proportions, and trying to protect her grandmother had made her beyond worldly. There was nothing she hadn't seen – well, nothing bad anyway. Artan, with his calm and deliberative manner had had a different life, steeped in nature, lonely maybe, but he hadn't seen what she'd seen. She liked the way he stroked the cattle, parental almost, and she liked the way he never wasted time, was always doing something useful, eyes intent on the job. Each were a victim of their past, but despite the age difference, there was an attraction which simmered, embarrassed them slightly, and caused the blood to run to their faces.

The house shook again under the gathering onslaught. Dog whined. Crow settled unhappily on a shelf, watchful eyes unblinking. They stared into each other's faces intently. Looking for solace, maybe hope, strength at least. There is strength to be gleaned through the eyes of another, if that other holds strong. That drawing from the communal well of fortitude required all participants to be a link in the chain of courage. Mother and son, woodsman and barbarian, they held the power of survival jointly and equally. If one weakened, the chain would break.

They should have been fearful, they should have been sleepless, but Ben and Minas lay close, relaxed and quiet, their fingers touching, casting a spell of sublime peace on the younger ones who snuggled into them. Dog, curled among the warm bodies, imbibed the contentment, eyes watchful.

The storm did not relent.

Nor did it the next day.

The Aftermath

Creeping out in the dying wind on the third day of the storm, it was easy to make a judgement. Trees down, rock falls, debris everywhere. A crinkled rusty motorbike, parts of a boat, mounds of plastic bottles. Much of this debris was useful, but first to check the animals.

Such a sorry sight. Minas looked away. Her beloved cows lay in a mangled heap, some were still moving. They were old, poor things, this was too much for them to survive. She spoke softly as she moved scattered branches from their broken bodies, trying to work out if any could be saved. Some already lay dead under a fallen tree, and they dragged the heavy bodies away. Some were too badly injured, and Minas despatched them with a long knife, talking to them, thanking them, loving them, tears running down her face. Ben took the knife out of her hand. "I'll do it. I don't know them. It'll be easier."

Out of the nine cows, only two survived. They were too old to give milk.

The bees had fared better. They had sensed the storm before it arrived, and most had returned home in good time. The boulders placed around the hive had stopped it from being blown about, but the bees would be unhappy with the disturbance, and their foraging was likely to be more meagre than usual as the few flowers around would have been ripped away. Minas calmed them by giving back some of their honey. It would strengthen them too.

The grisly task of salvaging what they could from the dead cows commenced. Dog and Crow couldn't believe their luck. Ben rebuilt the smoking shed whilst the boy, Minas and Barwin skinned and stripped the carcasses. There would be nourishing food for a few weeks to come, too much really.

It was hard, tiring work. The job had to be done quickly because although there were barely any flies, you could be sure that the ones there were would be on the meat in a shot. The knives constantly needed sharpening, their fingers ached. Every single bit of the dead cows had to be preserved and dried. For three days they were a veritable factory. Nothing else got done.

The smoking of the meat continued. There was enough green oak to keep the process going indefinitely, and Ben was relishing the job of chopping and chipping. It was a reminder of the old days, and he swiftly cleared away the offcuts into orderly piles for later perusal. By the end of one week, relative sanity had largely been restored, though the valley floor had lost its verdant serenity, devastated by the swollen stream, assorted detritus, and the gale. It would take a year to restore that.

Barwin became edgy. She had responsibilities. "I need to go back and find out if Gran is OK. You can spare me now, and I will have something decent to eat on the journey for a change."

Ben looked at Minas. He couldn't leave her. It would tear him apart. His pain at the thought was palpable. He had found his spiritual home in this gaunt older woman. He could only see beauty, and love and peace.

He couldn't leave her alone in this place, because he knew the sea, it's ways, the smell of it. He knew that if you sensed the storms, you would be too near to flee from them. It was the paradox of familiarity. The valley was not the safe place Minas craved, and he knew she would not move, not now, and he knew he would be with her, come what may.

Barwin smiled, she could sense what she could not put into words. Dog would be company enough.

They were all unprepared for the quiet treble voice of the boy, who looked up from the animal skin he was working on. "I'll go."

They all looked at Minas, who turned to look at her son, so very softly. All her aspirations and anxieties seeped bleeding out of her eyes. "Yes, you go. You can tell me about the world. Bring me something back."

It was a short goodbye, and it was their last. The next storm tore down the cottage wall and flung Ben and Minas into the wreckage of the falling roof as cliff boulders, anchored fast for millennia, dislodged and thundered down on them. Ben was trapped under a wooden beam too heavy for Minas to lift despite hours of desperate ingenuity. That inner drive, that visceral clutching for life, for his life, drove her to madness as her bloodied hands dragged stone after stone away in the teeming wet. She levered, fought the force of the hurricane, defied it to beat her as over and over again she mustered her most ferocious strength to free him. Her survival meant nothing without his.

Exhausted beyond endurance, she fell down beside him, cruelly beaten. Her long hair wafted across the face of the man she loved, and the wind ebbed. Crow, with feathers bent, lay broken at her side. Their last few hours together were the agony of days they would never have. Ben died first. She never left his side. A long, slow starvation did not cheat her.

Artan

The boy's name was Artan, after the constellation of Leo which was rising when he was born. His father had named him. Turkish, he had said. They trudged along the steeply winding track which led to the top of the valley. It was a path Artan knew well. Young though he was, he had ventured miles across the hinterland surrounding the valley. He told Barwin that he had watched them for all the days they had camped above the valley, scanning almost every move, checking their motive. He could have killed them, or at least one of them on several occasions, but he also knew that his mother was lonely, and needed some help with the constant tasks of scraping together an existence. That he loved his mother was not in dispute, but he was a boy who, at a young age, valued his independence. He was fortunate to have a mother who valued his sense of individuality.

"I think I'm like my dad," he confided. "Dad was a loner. Would go off for days, then come back with something amazing – like a walnut tree sapling!"

Barwin was too preoccupied with finding a trail back to where she came from to make much conversation. Reversing the angle of the sun, the position of rocks or bushes, the bogs and rivers, was hard enough in the best of circumstances, but since the storm there might have been changes, and any tracks they made were sure to be lost by now. She hadn't done a lot of tracking out in the open and was glad those wretched mountains were in view for most of the journey. She'd have to guess which pass to take over, so aimed for the twin peaks in the hope of passing between them.

When she realised they were crossing the remains of a dusty road, she knew her calculations had been faulty. Perplexing though it was – for they had not crossed a road on the outward journey – the centre of the road held a most mysterious object, large and brown, unmoving. Horse droppings! Quite fresh too. They ran quickly off the road to avoid being seen. Horses meant transport, this one could have been ridden, in which case it meant unknown humans. The road went from east to west across the moor. It was tantalizing, begging to be followed, but their way was south. They tried to map out the spot, but the devious moors gave little away in terms of landmarks, just a series of nondescript undulations, so they memorized what they could as Barwin kicked the dung into the edge of the road where it might do some good, sometime, maybe.

And there she had a revelation. Not of biblical proportions, but maybe much more significant. It was a tiny revelation, you had to be very close to notice it. Along the edge of the road, where the dust had gathered a few inches deep, tiny pieces of green were emerging. Hundreds of them, thousands, maybe millions. She beckoned Artan furiously, and together they sat down in speechless wonder. They put their faces to the ground, studied the minuscule green shoots, tried to work out what they might grow into, and simply marvelled at the spontaneous thrill of possible hope. Never before had they seen so many things at once striking out at life. She and the boy hugged each other in congratulation of everything, for here was the proof, the golden positive proof that anything was possible. You just had to stay alive long enough.

It must have been the hurricane, the winds stirring everything up, the wet, the humidity. Maybe these seeds came from another country, borne by the sea, whipped up into the heady vortices of a tempest a mile high and blown unceremoniously across the continents to be deposited on this sorry land.

A crushing hope, an impenetrable sadness, a cruel trick. Maybe. But there mingled the joy of what was, and grief at what might be. The two young figures were overwhelmed by everything at once, and they sat cross-legged on the edge of the road and wept.

From then on they didn't care that they had lost their way. Every step was an examination of potential new life. Even the scratch dry heathers and heaths looked to be softening. Barwin thought of the stubborn gorse bush which had helped her through those barren times, and begged the universe to favour humidity so that these gutsy little trail-blazers could have a chance of survival. It didn't matter for now what they were, whether they were food or poison, what mattered was their very presence.

She tried not to think too hard about the lessons her mother had given about biodiversity, how one species depended on the other, how everything was intrinsically linked together in the web of life and the health of one part was the health of it all. She tried not to think about the stirrings of miniscule life deep underground where insect and invertebrate might have burrowed, eking out their days of scant exactly as she had. She tried not to think about birds flying overhead catching insects in abundant skies, or ripening corn, or fruit trees or blackberries. She tried in vain. She knew that only a few days of blasting heat or cold would render all her dreaming hopes obsolete.

Whatever tomorrow would bring, their steps were faster now. A chink of optimism has a remarkable effect on the psyche. Sustained by the dried beef and fresh water from the weaving moorland streams, they eventually crossed the mountains, now pleasantly cool, and the lower landscape formed a familiar pattern which Barwin could follow. She thought it looked greener, but it was greener only in her hopes. Yet the rain had bestowed a general softening which the sun was inclined to enhance.

The journey took a day longer than the outward journey, and Barwin prepared herself for what she might find back at the carn. The old lady might not have made it through these last few weeks.

A Hairslide

A beautiful array of deep yellow flowers greeted her. The gorse bush was in full golden glory, on every branch. Its heady perfume wafted gently in the faint breeze and, for a moment, she felt drawn into its blissful enchantment.

And then the surprise. Shocking in its way. Barwin halted by the gorse bush in near stupefaction.

Children!

Yes, children!

Heads bent in concentration over some game scratched in the earth were two scruffy-headed children. Yet more shocking was the sight of Gran, sitting majestically on her favourite stone, arms around a little yellow-headed girl snuggled deep into her lap.

"Look what the wind's blown in!" she exclaimed cheerily when she saw her granddaughter, and the little ones looked up. "What a sight for sore eyes!"

"Where did they come from?" asked an incredulous Barwin, staring at the children.

"They just turned up, ever so hungry. You could have eaten a horse and chased the rider, couldn't you," she said, lovingly patting the little girl's hair. The little girl barely moved, a slightly vacant look in her eyes. The other children gathered round full of curiosity. "Who is your little friend?"

"Oh, this is Artan. A very useful person to have about the place," said Barwin, anxious to cover up the 'little' part of Gran's comment. Artan was, in the biggest sense of the word, to her, a man. He knew what a man should know, they had laughed and cried together, he was quiet and determined. A fellow survivor. Biologically speaking he might have a few years to go before he inherited the formal title, but his quiet interpretations of life were manly enough for her.

She went over and gave her gran a hug. This was indeed a sight for sore eyes. She'd half expected her gran to be dead. But here she was rosy with health and clucking contentedly as her brood gathered round her knees.

Gran was bubbling with excitement "I have a few surprises for you, Bar. They can wait, come and eat something, you must be hungry. Time and tide wait for no man."

It was clear that Gran could hardly wait to tell her tale, but they shared the dried meat, which was a sudden delight, and some lumpy broth from a pan suspended over the fire.

The two little boys quickly commandeered Artan. They wanted to know everything about him, preferably in ten seconds, and he, having not been with children before, was utterly bewildered by their eager jabbering and insistent hand pulling.

In a land of weird events, the story of how the children got to the carn was almost fantastic. The two boys had got lost on the moors running away from some thugs, when they spotted a large kite in the sky. They followed it as best they could, mainly because they had nothing else to do. They had never seen a kite before. It dipped over the moors, jettisoning some packages as it went. Born into scavenging as a way of life, they knew that these packages were probably worth something and hunted all day for them. A crow wheeled in circles over one particular spot, and to their amazement they found some quite large bags of corn. Some had split, and the crow was feasting away when they eventually found them. The boys couldn't carry all the bonanza, the corn tasted horrible, and they weren't sure what to do with it, but smoke was rising from a place not far away, and they resolved to use their unexpected bargaining power to gain maybe a meal or two.

"I was sending out smoke signals," giggled Gran, who had clearly been behaving as if she did not have a care in the world. Abandoned as she had been, she probably didn't.

The boys dashed to and fro, bringing in every last speck of corn they could find, scouting about the place and keeping their eyes open for anything unusual as Gran had bid. They were young enough for it all to be a great adventure, old enough to know where to leave the past. They absorbed each and every new idea entirely without question. For them tomorrow didn't particularly exist as a concept. In Gran they had found a relaxed mother figure who treated them almost as adults, and who fed them regularly. Work as play was a wonderful thing, and they would play as bandits and farmers all rolled into one – which was exactly what the situation required.

On one gallivanting foray they came across the little girl. They thought she might have fallen out of the kite like the corn. She was asleep and very, very cold. They half-dragged, half-carried her to Gran, thinking she might be dead.

Clutched close to Gran's soothing, but very diminished bosom, the little girl gradually recovered, but she wouldn't be parted from her source of love and warmth, for even a minute. Gran manoeuvred her round when she lay down, got up, cooked something or just sat and rested. The girl had not spoken a word since she was found.

"I don't know what her name is," said Gran, "but I call her Rosie.""That's a nice name, isn't it, Rosie?" she said, turning to the girl and fondling the knotted yellow hair. "We'll have to get a brush through this lot one day, won't we?" And the little girl just snuggled more closely.

Gran lifted the small knitted hat back from the girl's head. "There's something you should see, Bar." The girl quickly pulled her hat back down again, but not before Barwin had chance to see what lay pinned to her hair underneath.

It was incredible. So much so that Barwin felt she should see it again just to make sure. She tried to lift the hat, but the little girl would have none of it and hid her face in Gran's armpit.

"It's the same," said Gran, serious now. "Exactly the same."

How in all the world, the storms, the moors, the impossible lives that they all lived, could another identical hair slide even exist. Barwin reached to her own matted locks and pulled out the embedded hair slide.

"Sebastian," she thought. And her lively mind ran over ten thousand permutations of how this might have come to pass.

The child, Rosie, was clearly a victim of some kind of shock. She was locked in to her own self, possibly permanently. This level of trauma was not unknown. Barwin had seen it in the faces of both adults and children back in the towns. Inhumanity was as big a disease as the plague when food shortages became acute. Terrible things had happened, and people dealt with them in different ways.

The blank little face told no story. But the hair slide did. Barwin climbed down to the store to try and find the paper photograph which had been with the enamelled hair slide in Sebastian's pocket, the day she had cut the broken man down, that day, in the copse.

She had only kept it because it was a photograph, and she hadn't one of her own. Her own parents were a dim memory, slightly embellished by the passing sands of time. Her memory of her mother was probably more beautiful than reality, her father probably more handsome. What could not be erased was their courage and determination, which lived in her, fed her, informed her. Both passionate fighters against human excess and waste, avid campaigners against the monopoly of the corporations, they discussed most matters with their daughter, educated her in their science and the futility of continuous economic growth, the folly of extraction of minerals and metals, the damage that pesticides and herbicides were doing to the land and the precious little pollinators on which they all depended for something more than porridge. Her parents had kept a very productive kitchen garden which they tended daily. They taught her about storing seed for next year's crop, and how to grow the most beneficial plants and herbs both for pest control and for natural medicines. Fearing the worst, they also taught her how to use a gun.

The photograph of Sebastian's family group was brought out for study. There was a proud Sebastian, tall and smiling. Older people stood around him, and younger ones played in the foreground. A cheeky little girl was sticking her tongue out. Yellow hair. Barwin studied it. It was very likely to be Rosie. She took the photo over to Gran for her opinion, and the little girl clamped solidly to her lap turned one reluctant eye to see what they were talking about, and she stared, and stared.

Rosie

To tell Rosie's story accurately is not possible. She was too young to have an actual point of view. Her perspective as a slightly spoilt child could not see what was happening around her, only what was happening to her.

She was aware of a heightened anxiety in the household because the cook wasn't there, and neither was her friend the stable hand. Everything was very quiet. Her mum was in the kitchen and told her the cook had gone away for a few days. It was funny seeing her mum in the kitchen.

One night there was a lot of noise and some windows were broken. Someone attacked the house, and her mum told her to hide. She hid in a cupboard in the library and looked out through the keyhole. A man was sitting on her mum. Her mum was screaming and then a knife went into her. Her dad had a fight and ran out of the room. It went quiet, and Rosie went to look for her mum. Her body was lying on the floor like the dead calf she had seen. She was scared and went to look for her dad in the dark. There was a lot of horrible noise in the house, so she thought her dad might be in the stables. She couldn't find him. She was afraid to call his name in case the horrible people heard her.

She thought her dad might have gone to the woods to hide, so she went there, except it was dark and she got lost. She went to sleep sometimes when she was tired, but she didn't do that often in case her dad didn't see her.

Who knows how many days she had wandered without food and water. Who knows what she had actually seen. Her small pinched face spoke of nothing left to fear. Her silence reconciled.

Waldenby

It was inevitable.

They watched carefully as the new humidity in the air cosseted emergent green things, but once again Barwin was restless. A woman knowing the value of life dare not waste even an hour of time. She knew their food stocks at the carn were even less sustainable than those in the Valley, and it was time to set about replenishing them. There was no way of knowing what the moors would yield in these changing weather conditions, but the laws of nature dictated that most edible seeds would be found in old gardens. Waldenby was a vague hope.

Even if the tantalising green things grew into something edible, if they ever grew at all, it would be some weeks before they would mature, and even then they must leave plenty to go to seed for the following year. Chance had given them a chance. They had to nurture it carefully.

The boys, feral beyond fault, had to have the natural laws firmly embedded in their heads. They had to understand why they must be careful not to tread on young shoots, and then understand that they might not all be good to eat. Even an ant had to be respected because it was part of the overall food chain. The concept of biodiversity was explained in a rudimentary way, and they picked up on it quickly. Of course, every single living thing was dependent on every other single living thing. It made sense, like the song Gran sang to them about the old lady who swallowed a fly.

When the boys found a single thread of gossamer in the heathers, they ran to fetch Artan, and together they peered at the shimmering spectacle, were overjoyed to see a little golden spider, and plied Artan for more information on what spiders ate and what ate spiders.

Artan, who had eaten insects in the past, did not mention the nutritional value. There could be no compromise. Life had hung on by a thread the thickness of that silvery gossamer thread, and they must leave it alone at all costs.

And something else was happening. In the parched meadows below, not only was there a resurgence of grass, but little white specks had begun to appear. Artan knew about fungi too. The warmth and humidity had probably activated microscopic spores which had lain dormant for years. The mushrooms were their first totally fresh food, and again they left plenty to mature and spread spores anew.

It can be assumed that the last storm had been composed more of fresh water than salt; maybe it had brought seeds and dust from another land, maybe it had just activated what was already there, or maybe it was a heady mix of both. What was clear was that the new humidity had created perfect conditions for germination and growth.

Barwin packed her home-made rucksack, determined to find Waldenby alone. If she got into trouble it would be just too bad.

Dog wanted to follow her, but she knew this could be a dangerous move. Stealth might be required, and Dog simply could not contain himself when he came across an interesting scent. She told Dog to stay, and he definitely did not get the message, so she took him over to Gran. Rosie as always was on her lap.

Rosie, though not speaking, was listening intently. She slid down from Gran's lap and put her arms round Dog. He licked her face and allowed himself to be hugged. Rosie smiled. There is always room for a tiny miracle in everyday life.

Barwin said her perfunctory goodbyes, knowing that Artan was more than capable of looking after them all in the carn.

In fact, they were quite capable of looking after themselves without Artan. Rosie had given Gran something to live for, a new lease of life. The boys were quick and resourceful. Two hours after Barwin left, Artan followed her.

It was easy enough to track back to the road, and Barwin opted to go west because that's the direction, in logic, where Sebastian had come from. Not that logic was the best rule in these matters. She had no idea how many days he had been out on the moor. He had said that Waldenby was on Hensford Moor, a pretty good clue as the bulk of the moors went west. They quickly ran to lowland in the east.

The narrow road was deserted, no sign or sound of horses, but she kept away from it. Balmy nights made sleeping under the stars a pleasure, and she kept going until a river blocked her way. This fitted the topography Sebastian had briefly described. The river was small but deep, and the current ran fast. The redundant remains of a small hydro plant was lying idle nearby. It was a run-of-river type of arrangement where a portion of the river is channelled through a side canal. Sadly, it was not working. Possibly through lack of maintenance, or maybe some parts were broken. If it was the latter, the problem was pretty near terminal, for nobody was making spare parts for anything. And even if you had the tools to make them, you probably didn't have the raw materials. In the absence of maintenance, ingenuity could suffice. She was sure that hydro plant could be got working again. More hopefully, there was a wooden boat on the other side. "Useful," she thought, and memorised the layout of the land on the other side of the river, just in case.

She crossed the road which now veered to the north and followed it towards the mountains – the same range she had crossed what seemed like a lifetime ago. Life in the form of greenery was inhabiting the verges and the centre unmolested. It seemed this lane had not been used for a while. Stone walls, broken down, neglected, peppered the landscape and became her only cover. She began to feel exposed as the hummocks of the lower land gave way to windswept barrenness. A sense of foreboding stirred in her otherwise confident nature.

She took her time, pausing often to catch any sign of life, or the house. There was a clump of half-dead trees which looked hopeful, but she was apprehensive, and didn't want to go down.

Camping another night in the open, she decided to stay put and observe. Too far away to catch any noise, and with only her eyes and instincts for guidance, she waited. She felt sure this was the place, and equally sure it was inhabited. In the early morning she thought she heard a distant cock crow.

The house indeed was in those trees, and a sorry sight it was. Broken windows, falling walls, broken doors, gardens untended, greenhouse smashed. Its one-time splendour was only apparent from its size and layout. The warm honey-coloured stone walls were pockmarked with bullet holes. The once beautiful wisteria, once tended and lovingly trained around the windows, was now a battered dead wreck, hanging forlornly in parched brown tatters. Nine large windows adorned the front of the house, painted wooden shutters framed them, and the porch around the front door sported two grand marble pillars, themselves adorned with fragments of climbing roses which once would have filled the summer evenings with their heady perfume, the final remnants of a life lived with plenty.

The people who now commandeered Waldenby were rough, unruly, desperate. They ruled each other with violence and cruelty. If Barwin had known what was in store for her, she would have run.

But she didn't know. Her apprehension was strong, but her drive to find a better home was stronger.

She eventually had to break cover and find a way down to those trees; ducking and diving where she could, she ran down the hillside. Before she got close enough to verify her belief that the house was actually there, she got close enough to verify her misgivings.

Two of them, burly and uncouth, leapt out from what was clearly a masked lookout point. One on each side, they pulled her by the arms, threw her to the ground and sat heavily on her back. Resistance was pointless as well as impossible. She could do without broken limbs.

As soon as one plan is thwarted, another must immediately begin production. She would go passively with them, find out what she could, steal what she could, and get away.

Dragging her through the large door at the front of the house, she heard crude comments about her looks, her body. They pulled off her cap and played with her hair. One fondled her breast. She was disgusted.

They took her to what she believed was their leader. A large burly man of about thirty. He swore at her, forced her face towards his stinking mouth, and pushed his hand violently between her legs.

Paraded around what might once have been a baronial banqueting hall, they drew lots for who should have her first, second, third…

She was glad she wasn't a virgin.

Her shirt was ripped apart and she was bundled onto a bench, trousers pulled off, ripped over her boots. They pinned her down, one on each side, bruising her arms, splaying her legs, and she went limp. No point making a show of it. If she was tonight's entertainment, she wasn't going to give them the satisfaction of taking part. The first was mercifully quick. Her brain, stupefied, edited out the majority of the debauched language, the goading, the jeers.

Just the feeling of her vagina being thumped, and thumped and thumped remained. Someone grabbed at her hair, pulled her head back and masturbated into her face, revolting her, choking her. Satisfied with the damage, the first rapist shoved his fist into her vagina. Then the second. He took his time, bit her breast, hard, forced into her, hard, ripping the delicate skin of her vagina, bruising her raw, and on it went, on and on. The third, the fourth, her eyes were shut, she tried to take herself mentally away from the situation, she didn't know how many abused her, she didn't care. She expected she was bleeding. She passed out.

Conscious that she was being carried, slumped over someone's back, she saw stairs coming into focus beneath her, then she was dumped on a floor. The door slammed shut. And locked.

Kind hands bathed her face, but she was not ready to face reality, kind or cruel.

Soothing words, a female voice.

Possibly hours later she opened her eyes. Sore and stiff, she looked around. Three other women were in the room. One was brushing the long dark hair of another, sitting straight-backed and statuesque on the floor. The third was bending over Barwin, smiling in a motherly fashion.

Barwin was feeling too bruised and grumpy to smile back. Her ordeal infuriated her. She wanted a future free from fear and misogyny, and yes, she would like to kill every one of those foul slathering men who had abused her. Anger, far from subsiding, was increasing. She swore and cursed and clenched her fists. Vengeful hate consumed her fighting spirit until she ran out of expletives and common exhaustion took over.

"They'll leave you alone for a while now," came the reassuring voice leaning over her, gently combing through the knots in her outrageously unkempt hair. "For a while..." thought Barwin, bristling at the thought that this was likely to happen again. She had to get out.

Rising awkwardly to her elbows, she took a look at the room. There was a picture of a girl in a blue dress hanging on the far wall, a bow in her hair, hands resting gently in her lap. Someone had scribbled a huge penis between her hands.

The walls were pale blue, the windows were barred, a dirty mattress was on the floor. "This," she thought, "was Sebastian's luxury home. It's come to this. Maybe Sebastian did the right thing."

The two other women came over, smiling, probably through their own pain, mistakenly thinking that calmness was what was needed.

"How do I get out of here?"

The lady with the sleek black hair smiled again. "We can't. The door is locked, the windows barred, and when we do go out, there are always two of them to restrain us."

"How long have you been here?" demanded Barwin, a little too sourly.

"Me?" responded the woman with the sleek black hair, almost guiltily. "Weeks, I suppose. The others were here before I came."

Barwin looked accusingly at the other two, as if they should have died in an escape attempt the day they arrived. She was bitter. Trapped. She wasn't bred for captivity. She needed a bath or a swim to get the vile stench of those men out of her.

"We do have a sort of plan," said the older lady with dishevelled curly hair. "I'm Ellie, by the way, and this is Nina, and this is Blue. We call her Blue because she was that cold when she arrived I thought she would die."

Barwin, at that moment, didn't actually care what they were called. She gave her name to be at least civil, and asked Ellie to go on.

"There is one man who is a bit different from the others. Not so keen on rape, more intelligent, maybe a bit thoughtful. We think he's putting on a show to be accepted by the others. We're working on him to let us work in the garden. He's called Adam."

"Do you know anything about gardens?" asked Barwin, vaguely interested in the plan, not that there was any choice, for now.

"Not a lot," Ellie replied. "But enough to blag it through."

Ellie had been a schoolteacher, working mostly with ten-year-olds. Her marriage was childless, and made bearable by the love she held for all her charges. She had insisted the school set aside a patch of garden so that the children could learn how to grow and tend fruit and vegetables. She learned as they learned, her prim countenance always concerned that the future was unlikely to be like the past. She knew about global warming in a rudimentary way, and was determined her children should understand the very basics of survival – at least when it came to food. She fussed around her little ones, shared their wonder when the tiny harvest was made and tried to get the parents interested. It was her small contribution to the real future. In fact, it was the only useful lesson those children ever had.

Her pretty blond hair had given way to several inches of grey at the roots. The hairdressers had gone out of business overnight. No power, no supplies, and in the manic dash for survival, having your roots touched up was the last thing on anybody's mind.

From a society concerned with the way people looked, dressed and wore their hair, she had plunged headlong from a full wardrobe of neat suits, twinsets and pearls, down to the clothes she stood up in the day the hurricane struck four long years ago. Her dainty little pussy-heeled shoes were replaced with somebody else's trainers, her skirt replaced with looted jeans, her unseemly grey hair roots were disguised with a stylish beret. She joined the black market in purloining what she could, selling what she could and bartering what she couldn't. Ellie was the type of person for whom 'keeping up appearances' was very important, and she did just that. From primary school teacher to ruthless negotiator in a matter of weeks, she was resourceful, for as long as the vestiges of her world held out, which it didn't. Picking off the last of her chipped nail varnish, she ventured among the plague victims to scavenge what she could. She held herself above the horror of it all until she could bear no more, and prepared to die; she could see no other escape. Sitting forlorn on a street corner, a random encounter with another survivor gave her just enough will to carry on a bit further. They kept house together for a while, someone's house, and had a most respectable few months acting like an ordinary suburban couple, creating for themselves a ludicrous order in the nightmare. Then the mobs came to their street. He was killed, she was captured. Her ability to create a reasonable meal out of very little kept her alive. She cooked for the gang, and they spared her life. She mothered them, knowing that cruel and ruthless though they were, they too were traumatised. It was a precarious existence, but in her mind they became her 'children', her class of ten-year-olds, and they developed a weird affection for her as she tidied and folded their clothes, told them to clean their teeth, and generally became a symbol of order amongst the insanity of their world.

It all changed when she got to Waldenby. Out of place in the unforgiving wastes of the countryside, the gang forgot they needed her trifling touches of kindness to keep them remotely human. They locked her away, occasionally remembered to feed her. In her absence the gang deteriorated under a new, more brutal rule, and started collecting people. Nina joined her, then Blue. She thought they might be needed for procreation purposes, because the gang was all male. But she misjudged them. They hadn't thought that far ahead.

Barwin warmed slightly. In her anger she might have underestimated them.

"When do we get some food?"

"Who knows. But we'll get something, sometime, probably."

They did. Some revolting gristly leftovers mashed up on a plate.

That night they slept together across the width of the mattress, their feet hanging over the side. Sardines in a tin. Women in mutual agony. Slaves to a debauched regime from which there appeared to be no immediate escape. Mixed emotions, always mixed emotions. The abuse of one usually meant the others had been bought a few hours of respite. The abuse of one though, was abuse of them all. Arms around each other they took solace in the human warmth and kindness kindled by their mutual suffering.

Barwin was unfamiliar with the feel of body warmth coming from such close quarters, but she slept.

The sun rose through the morning mist. Barwin flinched as she moved her legs. She cursed at her oppressors.

Wincing, she went to look out of the window. There were gardens all right, just as she imagined, and a tatty sight they looked. Bare and brambly, they could once have been the kitchen garden for the house. She wanted to meet this Adam who could be instrumental in her escape, but the bright morning light seemed to enable her to see more clearly into the situation. They had been making plans, and she should not be interfering unless invited.

She lay back on the bed. Sitting was out of the question. She stared at the picture. Nina was lying beside her, shiny black hair defying grimy reality. "Modigliani," she said. "It's called Alice."

Barwin was a bit amazed that someone knew the name of the painting, and its painter, and asked Nina how she knew.

"I was an art historian, once." Barwin could just about imagine that. Sleek Nina, willowy and pale, with an amazing job in a gallery or somewhere cool and sophisticated, where the air barely stirred when you moved, and where enormous amounts of money changed hands. She could see Nina, wine glass in hand, designer cocktail dress making her look even slimmer than she actually was, holding court at the opening of an exhibition, talking intimately to a potential buyer about the most fashionable artists, beguiling the art world with her intelligent smile and depth of knowledge. She could see Nina in the rarified atmosphere of silent paintings, beautiful people and weighty bank accounts. Nina, and those like her, would have fallen the farthest, yet to look at her natural poise and hear her elegant speech was to think she hadn't fallen at all. To Nina, this was just a lull in proceedings. Do not adjust your set because normal service will be resumed as soon as possible.

This life was only possible for her as long as she held on to the thought that this whole debacle was simply an unfortunate interim event. For her, van Gough and Picasso were just waiting in the wings.

"Modigliani painted all these long-faced women." She continued in her slow drawl, certain of her facts. "He adored them. He pretended he was an alcoholic and a drug addict to hide symptoms of an infectious disease. In his day drunks were tolerated, infectious diseases were not."

"What was his disease?" asked Barwin, brain racing.

"Tuberculosis. It's an infection of the lungs. Very infectious. Spreads from one person to another through tiny droplets in coughs and sneezes."

"Could we get it? I mean, could we pretend to have something infectious which would make them leave us alone."

"They'd probably kill us," interjected Ellie, feet, as ever, firmly on the ground.

Barwin was not giving up. "But how about we have something which was bad for them, but still let us do the gardening?"

"Venereal disease," said Blue quietly. "I think I've got it. I also think I'm pregnant."

"Oh God," said Ellie, who might have thought there was one, and they instinctively reached for each other's hands.

Barwin didn't know what venereal disease was, but she knew about pregnancy. They lay there quiet. The four of them.

The Plot

Like the flip sides of a coin, many things come in pairs. Like adventure and trouble. These aspects bring challenges, yet many need a balance of both. The problems start when one overrules the other. That's when life swings to an extreme.

They had all been screwed by the same men. Disease for one was potential disease for all. Barwin received a quick education.

It was by no means certain that Blue, or anyone else for that matter, had any form of sexually transmitted disease. The symptoms could just as easily be caused by poor hygiene, and in their case, with a shortage of clean water, there was practically no hygiene. Blue said she had vaginal itching, and was understandably worried. She had kept it to herself for a long time, and it had grown and festered in her mind. Neither could she be absolutely certain that she was pregnant, but the best course of action was to keep her away from the most violent men, and, in the absence of antibiotics – which barely worked anyway since most bacteria had made themselves immune through random mutation, natural selection, and over prescription in the bad old good old days – the best plan, indeed the only plan, was to simply forget about STD in personal terms, but use the idea of it to their advantage.

Blue, a woman of few words, had been an athlete, a champion for her country. Not that it mattered these days. Emaciated though she might now be, her body retained the strength and determination instilled over many years of arduous training. A triathlete, robust. A swimmer, a cyclist and a runner, she had survived the years since the disaster by being constantly on the move. Grabbing what she could to stay alive, always alone, her mental capacity to outsmart adversity had served her well. Until of course she, like everyone else on the outskirts, was driven to search wider afield, to make unsteady alliances with strangers. Sex was the only commodity she had left to barter. It no longer mattered who with. Staying alive was the primary concern.

Blue alone had been having very light, barely noticeable periods. Menstruation had stopped for the others as malnutrition set in. That anyone under the circumstances of the last few years could retain the remotest possibility of fertility was extraordinary. No one had seen a pregnant woman, or a baby born for years. That one of their number might be having a baby was little short of a miracle. Most of the children running around were more than five years old. Blue saw it as an added encumbrance to her pathetic existence. Ellie, who had lost her own children at birth, saw it as the most wonderful thing possible, and clapped her hands and cried with happiness. Nina, younger, but childless, had mixed feelings, and Barwin was deeply in awe.

They had to protect her.

The room, being part of a once almost stately home, had many rooms panelled to waist height. Most of them were oak, and had been painted over. Barwin pulled at some of the panelling in a corner, and it was giving, slightly. She needed something to use as leverage. The old house was probably built of crumbly mortar and brick, and if she could make a way into the next room, which seemed to be empty, they would at least have the start of a means to escape. She tried prising at it with a metal spoon. It bent.

In her view, she and her unhappy companions were entirely expendable. It was the unutterable fact of their lives. They were extra mouths to feed, and kept only for recreation. "I am not going to die here," she whispered to herself with some finality. She went over to the window and studied the shutter fixings. Strong pieces of ironmongery much too sturdy for the job they were currently employed for. Just reachable through the bars but not rotten enough to make the job easy, they were all she could think of. The spoon could be used as a screwdriver, so she worked away.

Keys jangled in the lock and the door opened briskly. Barwin stepped away from the window. A swarthy man stomped across the room and grabbed Blue by the arm.

"She's not well," said Ellie.

"Who cares," muttered the man and hauled Blue up from the bed.

"We think it's contagious."

The man stalled. "You'll do." and he dropped Blue and grabbed Ellie.

Back at the window, Barwin could see a lone black bird gliding on the thermals overhead. She wondered why her captors did not shoot at it. Maybe they had no bullets. She thought of Crow.

"Not too bad," said Ellie on her return in answer to the enquiring glances. "And I've managed to get us another bucket of water."

Quiet jubilation greeted the entrance of a plastic bucket filled with rainwater. Now they had a bucket to wash in, one to drink from, and one to defecate in. First they drank, then they decanted some for future use, then they washed their faces and hands. What was left was given to Barwin to wash out the blood and sperm from the day before. "That one was called Nuke. I mentioned about the garden. I'm not sure what the grunt he replied with meant."

By the end of the day, Barwin had worn her fingernails bloody, but one shutter fixing was off. Pointed at one end, it could be quite a useful tool.

The door banged open again, and Nina was taken out. With an elegantly defiant air, she walked with her head held high, proud and graceful, as if born to aristocracy. In every way a thoroughbred, slim boned and long-legged, with a touch of the orient about her dark eyes, it was as if she belonged to another world, unfettered by mere flesh and blood, unconcerned by the everyday affairs of ordinary mortals.

She left the room as graceful as a swan. She returned a broken child. Doubled over, blood running down her face and legs. Blue and Ellie rushed to comfort her.

"Blad," she whispered.

They all knew Blad. He was a pervert and a sadist. Anal sex was his preferred option, before and after he had beat you senseless. Unfortunately, he had taken a liking to Nina. He enjoyed beating this beautiful woman into submission.

Barwin couldn't bear to look. The obscene malice and violence evident in the attack on Nina had reduced this exotic creature almost to a pulp. She didn't complain, she didn't cry, she didn't speak. She just lay on the filthy mattress in a foetal position, arms clutching at her ribcage, whilst the others gently bathed her with rags and stale water. None of them spoke. None of them had the vocabulary for this. Each in their own private thoughts, each with tears of hopelessness and compassion and love, they softly brushed her hair and cleaned her wounds. There was no medicine, spiritually or physically, for this.

Unable to cope with the scene, Barwin laboured away at the panelling. She had to make sure it did not splinter so that no evidence of her work could be seen. As she worked she reassessed her journey to Waldenby, her state of mind. She had not been confident about her decision to come here, yet the idea, encouraged by the sight of the other little hair slide seemed to point the way. In any case the options were limited. Either she tried Waldenby, or somewhere completely unknown, which might yield worse than nothing. Every journey had its hazards, and she had been lucky up until now. At any rate she controlled her own luck to some extent with that watchful gaze, that patience, that ability to discern what was useful and what was not, when to move on and when to stay. She had seen enough, learnt enough, to survive thus far. What she had avoided, as much through planning as good fortune, was the brutal incarceration she was now experiencing.

Hours of stoic determination crept by, punctuated only by the silent whimpering of Nina. Gently, gingerly, she prised a section of panelling away from the wall.

"Right," she announced. Unaware of how much mental strength she had at her disposal. Unaware of the power in her demeanour. Barwin didn't usually give out orders because there had never been anybody around to actually give orders to. She 'managed' Gran, who was happy to go along with any suggestion, because she trusted her granddaughter implicitly, despite her shortage of years. And anyway, Gran couldn't manage her way out of a paper bag if left to her own devices. It was her grandmother's strength that she knew this. Of one thing Barwin could be sure, she didn't want to be in the position where any of these foul-breathed monsters were controlling her life. She needed to control the situation, even for a little while. Helplessness was not her style. Leaving matters in the hands of destiny was not an option.

Thus, after a period of reflection, she began to make confident decisions about what should happen next. Her mental strength returned, and with it, the diminishment of her physical pain.

"That has to stay on the wall at all times," she indicated to the piece of panelling she had been working on, "except when we are working on it. I think we can shift one of the bricks and start to make a hole big enough to climb through. We hide the rubble under a floorboard. I'll lift one in a bit."

They took it in turns to work at the wall, a rattle at the door gave them just enough notice to push the panel back before one of the men came in. It was painstakingly slow. No dust or mortar must be allowed to show at any time.

Then Adam came for Barwin.

She hadn't recovered from the gang rape, could barely walk without the internal soreness making her wince. Now she knew why the others hadn't managed to escape, they were too sick and injured. She was mortified at her previous attitude towards her abused roommates.

Adam took her into another equally decrepit room across the passageway, locking the door behind him. He pointed to his hair. "Look," he said, "I'm ginger like you."

Barwin wasn't at all sure what that had to do with anything. She stood there quiet, dreading.

"I reckon we gingers ought to stick together. What do you think?"

She wondered if he was a little bit simple. Thought it best to humour him. He hadn't lunged at her, or made any advances, weird or otherwise. His face was young, fragile even. Maybe he was in his twenties, maybe younger. It was hard to tell. His clothes fitted badly, and he had a habit of flicking his hair back from his face with a twitch of his neck, then pulling it forward again with his hand.

She studied him in that calm and level-eyed way she had. The way she evaluated the odds in a difficult situation. Her inner voice was searching for a reason to trust him. She called upon her deepest wisdom for guidance. His tone was insistent, childlike, honest. It was the way he leaned in to her, trusting her, clutching at straws maybe, but there was desperation in his eyes.

She nodded. Tried a smile. Failed.

"I'm going to trust you because you're ginger, and you look smart. I need to get out of here, really fast. When they find out I'm gay, they will probably kill me, or worse. I can't keep the pretence up much longer. The terrible things they do to these women, the things I have to join in with. I just can't do it. I just can't take it…" His voice trailed into a sobbing desperation.

Well, they said they thought he was a bit different.

"What's your plan?" Being direct was both her main attribute and her main fault.

He shook his head.

Barwin had had enough of people not having decent plans, so she made one up, based on what the others had said, just to keep him talking.

"You get two of us working in the garden, so we can be outside without causing suspicion. I'll work on getting the other two out of the house. Then we need a commotion of some sort to act as a distraction. A really big one, like burning the house down. We'll have worked out the best escape route by then. "

"Can you make some noises, please. Like you're in pain or something. They might be listening."

She made appropriate noises, he joined in. In that peculiarly amusing moment, they smiled at each other, and a tenuous bond was formed.

She repeated her plan to him, and he was interested. He was desperate. She congratulated herself. Here was someone on the inside who was in the much same situation as her; at least they both wanted to escape, which was all the common ground needed.

He had no idea how he was going to persuade the others to get the women working in the garden, but Barwin carefully explained about the green shoots, that the brutes were going to need a supply of food, and that gardens need tending daily if they are to produce anything useful, and that they all knew something about gardening.

He warmed faintly to the idea.

"What have you got to lose by trying it?"

"OK, I'll try it, but it will have to be quick."

He had not said what was really on his mind, for they had run out of food a while back. The occasional deliveries by homing kite, enabled through radio contact with other groups, had not come through for weeks. There was some kind of master plan in which all the connected groups would subdue potential rivals and prop up each other's petty kingdoms. The future world would have forgotten about land ownership, or at least who owned what land, and these groups would lay claim to all. History repeating itself. The Robber Barons staking out the land and defending it with bloody force. Waldenby had been earmarked as a good semi-fortified stronghold. But these were urban thugs: they did not know how to tend the land or look after livestock. They did not even have the gumption to maintain their outer defences. This group was particularly inept, partly due to belligerent thuggery, partly due to incompetence.

Just like every other tentative community trying to knit themselves together, their main preoccupation was sustenance in terms of food. They were permanently disgusted with oats and grains; what they wanted was meat. A horse hanging round the periphery was caught and horribly butchered. They had no idea what they were doing. Ignorance and blind to the suffering they were inflicting, the poor thing took hours to die. Poor housekeeping and lack of knowledge caused the majority of this slaughter to be wasted.

Possibly the other groups no longer had a surplus, possibly they were defunct through disease or infighting or starvation. Either way the reality on the ground for this group was one of getting food. They had raided and pillaged in the past, but out here on the moors there was nothing much to raid or pillage. By contrast, Barwin's great triumph had been her struggling journey. She travelled light, moved when she should – either through outside factors or inner need – stolen when she needed to, and stubbornly stayed on the outside of the unhappy crowd. Like a true barbarian she would bother no one unless she had to, and kept herself quiet and discreet, hidden within the scenery of town or country. No one knew she was there, or anywhere. She did not exist. It was her chosen liberty. Until now.

This grotesque, sub-human group wanted to stay and build their own petty kingdom where they were, picking up survivors and using brutality to keep order. It might have been dawning on them that staying at Waldenby was not sustainable, but even that matter was being brutally resolved. Thus, the agony tormenting Adam's mind was what they were eating, now.

Barwin was troubled by his high state of anxiety, fearing it would undermine any escape attempt, no matter how thorough the plan. "If we rush it, they will suspect something, Adam. You need to work on this over time, though any time is too long for us."

"Then we need another plan," pleaded Adam. "Do you know what we are eating?"

Barwin looked bemused.

"We are eating us. We are the only food. You girls and people like me who don't fit in are the larder."

It took a moment for this to penetrate Barwin's brain.

Her mouth slipped slightly open, her eyes stared out in horror. Horror of horrors.

Cannibalism.

The scraps they had been eating which they joked over because none of them could identify what they were.

Revulsion.

Shock.

Human meat.

They had been eating human flesh.

She quelled the rising lurch in her stomach. "Right. Quick is good. Maybe we should all just make a run for it. Can you get hold of knives, weapons of any sort? Animal traps? Pitchforks even? When's the best time? Night. Is night the best time?"

"I'll get what I can. Everything is locked and barred at night."

"Right." She felt she should take control, if only her self-control would reassert itself. "Right." She couldn't think properly. "Right." The horrible taste in her mouth was getting more profound, saliva sticky, was trying to combat the rising acid in her stomach. "Right. I'm going to be sick." And she was violently sick, dredging up what little there was in her stomach. Retching until her eyes practically forced their way out of her head.

Adam forced her head between her knees. "Don't tell the others. They might panic."

Barwin nodded, head spinning. They had to get out. To stay any longer might well cost another life, and who knew which one they would choose. It could be her.

Recovering slightly, she announced with some finality, "We'll go tonight, might as well die escaping as any other way. Blue and Nina are too weak to put up much of a fight, but Ellie, you and I could. Get some weapons, disable what you can't carry. Where is the weakest part of the house? How do we get to it?"

The work in the corner of the room was going well. The shutter hinge, with its pointed end, made the job fairly easy. Three bricks had been dislodged and hidden under the floorboards. Two more bricks and they would be able to get through.

Barwin was escorted suitably roughly into the prison room by Adam. Their sisterly enquiring eyes were met with surprising brightness despite the red rimming her swollen eyes.

"It's OK, really. You said he was different. He is."

She told Ellie, Blue and Nina they were leaving that night. Had they protested she would have told them why, but they did not. Even Nina, who was in considerable pain and could barely walk, was in agreement. They had been in captivity longer than Barwin; their will to leave was at least as strong as hers. She explained that she and Adam had forged a plan, and gave an outline. An outline was barely what they had anyway, but it is not difficult to persuade a person who needs no persuading.

Artan, alone, outside the perimeter walls of the house, had seen the two men capture his friend, and was agitated. Living as he had in the quiet valley devoid of human life except for his loving mother, he had not come across any level of human brutality, but instinctively he knew the situation was not good. He was waiting for the opportunity to move further towards the house. Crow was circling above him. He had seen Barwin at the window and his keen eyes caught the movement of others in the same room.

Barwin had previously shown him the small treasures she stored back in the carn, among them were the set of keys which came out of Sebastian's pocket. As he packed a few things ready to follow her, he thought of the keys. Waldenby would have lockable doors. They might be useful, if indeed they found Waldenby.

Thus, on a windy night when all inside was silent, he crept round the house trying the keys in every door. One at the back worked.

His keen eyes had also noticed the fledgling flora of the kitchen garden. That which was not completely dead was tentatively putting forth tender shoots and leaves. He ate mint, and marjoram, dandelion leaves and grass. It supplemented the few strips of dried meat in his bag. He deduced that the dormant seed of many a vegetable was in a precarious uprising. Brambles were in flower. Good for here, maybe good for everywhere. A new hope replaced his feelings of desperation. Old gardens across the land might be swelling in growth. He envisaged a future of seed barter, salvation, survival.

A few chickens had escaped the butcher's cleaver. He found their nest in an old hedge far from the house, impossible to find unless you knew what to look for. In it were fifteen eggs. It was not possible for him to tell how old they were, but the one he ate was fresh enough. He wrapped seven up in a shirt, and left seven for the hens, thanking them for the favour. There was no sign of a cockerel, but he thought he had heard a cock crow on the first morning in these parts. If indeed there had been a cockerel, the eggs might be fertilised. He reasoned that in this case they might make the beginnings of a new homestead.

The following night was clear-skied. The crescent moon shed just enough light for him to see where he was going. He crept round the walls, looking for a weak point. His aim was to enable a swift escape route to the river where he had ensured the wooden boat was watertight enough for his purposes, moved it, and hidden it.

Skulking silently round the outbuildings he heard guttural voices, muffled noises, scuffling. Ducking out of sight, he saw three men dragging another out to where the kitchen garden once was. The one being dragged was protesting, violently, with every limb, dragging his legs and clutching at anything within reach. His hands were roughly prised off walls and sticks. He was gagged, but he was screaming, desperately, you knew it. He was thrown to his knees, and you could tell he was begging, pleading, beseeching. The two held him down, the third pulled his head back by the hair and cut across his throat with a knife. Choking, gurgling noises filled the air, cruel enough to haunt your every dream. As with the horse, it was not done well. The gurgles continued for minutes. It seemed like hours. Artan had witnessed his first cold- blooded murder.

We're surrounded by invisible energies. Waves of light, heat and radio constantly pass through our bodies. Quantum particles are constantly speeding through us.

Science has yet to prove that that lines of energy exist between people and places. But at times we feel something almost electric, and it informs our deeper consciousness. Times of deep love, disaster, distance, sometimes connect people and animals in a unique way. Birds too. Crow, adopted by Minas as a fallen fledgling had rarely left her side. It was a natural imprint. A baby bird does not know what she is, so she visually imprints herself with her mother. It is a survival mechanism, and when young birds imprint on humans, they identify with humans for life. Crow was bonded to Minas for life. She identified with humans in preference to her own species.

It cannot be known why Crow had left Minas, but for sure she identified with Artan almost as closely. Maybe she thought of him as a potential mate, or a sibling, or maybe there was a completely different driver. Maybe her strange avian nature compelled her to hunt with him, to watch over him. Or maybe she perceived that the magnetic field connecting Minas and Ben was too strong for her to intrude upon.

When Barwin next looked out of the window it was to scout, with her eyes, the perimeter wall. She had done it before, but this time it was urgent to pick the right place, preferably on the river side. If they actually made it alive out of the house, getting clear of the wall was at least as vital.

The drifting bird caught her eye, again. This time she knew, without question, that it was Crow. Why was she here? Gripped by an intense and unexpected emotion, her understanding leapt across the divide. Artan was here. He was always here. She sensed it. In that moment a fundamental and lasting link between these two young people was cemented. She knew he could see her. She waved. She tried to motion that tonight they were going to make a break for it. She hopped about like a madwoman. Artan was here. He might only have looked like a ten-year-old boy to some, but he was her inspiration.

Just one hundred metres away, and she could not see him, but the charged particles in the air ran between them in a line of pulsating energy. He could see her.

Day turned to dusk, and the sun burned red. The four women sat in agitated contemplation, aware that if any of the thugs came for them tonight, they would be left behind. That was the agreement. The hole in the wall was big enough to get them through one at the time. Ellie had put her head through earlier, and the door to that room was open. One less mountain to climb.

Loud voices at the door. They froze. Blad. Nina stared at the window. She would have thrown herself out if it had not been barred. But life, or even death, is not that easy.

Escape

Blad slammed the door open, looked at Nina prostrate on the bed, threw his head back and laughed as if he found her plight comedic. He held his arms out and swayed round the room as if asking for applause. It was clear from the twisted grin on his face that yet more cruelty was on his mind. The door locked shut, and he took three steps towards the cowering woman. Barwin had the pointed shutter hinge in her hand. It was a reflex. It certainly was not planned. It felt to her like slow motion. She moved silently across the room, raised her arm, and plunged the hinge into his back with enormous force, just as he was bending down to grab Nina's arm. He turned around in surprise.

"Oh shit," muttered Ellie, who by now was behind the hated oppressor, and who realised it would take more than this to kill a large man, quickly, anyway.

She pulled the hinge out roughly, stepped back and plunged it in again using both arms for extra force. He bent over slightly, a bemused look on his face.

Blue, seizing the initiative, pulled his legs from under him, and he landed on the mattress next to Nina, blood coming out of his mouth. She stuffed a cloth into his mouth to stop him shouting. They all stared for a moment, unsure what to do next, then Nina, face to face with her torturer on the mattress, coldly clasped her finger and thumb across his nostrils. The others held his arms down. It took forever for him to suffocate. Nina held her nerve. It was not revenge, it was just what had to be done.

Barwin had not agreed to meet Adam until it was dark, the timing was all wrong. Unable to forgo habits of old, she went through Blad's pockets even as he was dying. Odd that he should have a cigarette lighter. She didn't even give herself time to consider it a miracle. She took his knife and his belt. She pulled the hinge out of Blad's back.

It was time to seize the moment. This was the only moment they would have.

"Change of plan, girls! We go now. Come on, now!"

They scrabbled through the opening behind the panel, hauling Nina through though the pain was clear in her face. Then Barwin scrabbled back again.

Fire. She had asked Adam to create a diversion by setting something on fire. She couldn't wait for Adam. Quickly she tried to set the mattress on fire. It smouldered. She went to the window and lit the torn edge of what was left of the curtains, with better luck. She hoped Artan would see it.

Running round the room, she gathered their few rags, lit them, and stuffed them partly under the wooden panel. It was all she could do. There was no time to see if her work was good.

The next room had more combustibles. Barwin set fire to everything. Blue knew the layout of most of the upstairs rooms and led them silently to the disused back of the house. Through the gloom they peered through the windows, looking for a shelf or a lower roof. Two rooms later they found one, but in a high-ceilinged house the drop was dangerously long. Blue volunteered to jump and scout the next move.

They heard noises, they smelt smoke. Blue disappeared along the lower roof. The wait was interminable. The noises nearer.

"Those bloody women," they heard. "Told you we should have killed them first."

"Wouldn't have had so much fun," retorted another.

"Where the hell are they?"

Doors were banging open and shut.

It was getting too close. They shrank away from the window and pressed themselves against the door. Hearts pounding.

"Kaa, kaa" came a noise from below. Like a crow it sounded, but there was only one crow around here and she never made a noise.

Artan! Barwin rushed to the window, she could see nothing, but the bird call sounded again; it was coming from below, and to the right.

"Kaa, kaa" she responded in hope.

Just then Blue came back. "I can't find a better way down, you'll have to jump."

"Make for the sound of the crow, Blue, it's a friend." If Blue had time to process this, it would not have made sense, but they were acting on blind impulse; rationality was replaced by the adrenaline rush of flight or die.

Barwin fastened the buckle of the newly deceased Blad's belt to the handle on the window. It might hold, for a bit. She let the long end of the belt hang down. It gave them a few feet less to fall. She motioned to Nina.

"I can't," Nina said simply, still clutching her chest, her head shaking in sorrow. "I'll try another way inside when they have gone to other rooms. My ribs…"

No time to remonstrate. Barwin went down first, Ellie was to follow. The door burst open. Ellie paused just long enough to see someone grabbing Nina by the throat, and the moral rectitude of this prim school teacher from a long dismembered suburbia, did not hesitate.

"Oh, no you don't!"

She ran to protect Nina, to stay his hand. Before she reached her a knife was thrown. It hit Ellie squarely in the chest, stopping her dead, plain dead.

Barwin could not wait. Flames were sprouting from the windows on the other side of the house. Adam had come good.

Blue had found Artan on the kitchen roof. Barwin found Adam in the flames. The four of them jumped through an open skylight, careered through the unlocked back door, and out through a side garden to the opening in the wall made by Artan.

The only thing that mattered was to get to the boat, and they ran desperately. The evening was not dark enough to hide them; they could only count on the surprise of the house being on fire. They ducked and dived, hidden for a while by the great wall, then ran flat out to the river. Only when Artan had pushed the boat away from the side of the bank with a tree branch, did they sink down and draw breath. The current took them into the centre of the river, and as it drifted, they turned back to see the ghost of Waldenby blazing in the evening sky.

The River

A girl of fifteen, a boy of ten, a pregnant woman and a homosexual man. It was indeed a motley crew which drifted down the little river all that night. They had youth and vigour, knowledge and insight – the makings of a community. What they lacked in luck they could make up with ingenuity, and in that positive frame of mind they shared their dreams.

Adam had been a happy kid, good at schoolwork and loved by his family. He knew he was homosexual almost all his life, and his parents were completely at ease with the fact. Homosexuality was far from unusual in the 2020s and he grew up in a world which embraced diversity, for the most part. There were pockets of discrimination in certain parts of society, but he never came across them. It was only when the triple catastrophes of hurricane, virus and climate change poured their malice on the population that he experienced his first homophobic attack. All the old prejudices crawled out of the woodwork. The disabled were ridiculed, their wheelchairs and crutches smashed, the old and weak were pushed around; too scared to go out, they locked their doors and starved to death. Homosexuals of any gender became targets and were hunted down, dismembered and left to die – and that was before the real backlash started. Adam had never been in a closet of any kind, but he found one very quickly. A life of pretence and forced masculinity was his only hope. He became part of the gang warfare, all the time trying to prove his fake masculinity to his brutal peers. The stress was immeasurable. He killed people, jeered along with the rest as women were robbed and raped, he stole and smashed along with the worst of them, and ended up with the Waldenby gang in a state of near suicide. With the arrival of Barwin, her red hair and his desperation were the only catalysts he needed to try and make a break for it. His only dream was to be left alone to be himself.

Blue had known fame if not fortune. Her world of sport and discipline disappeared almost as soon as the lights went out. Her family had all been lost to the Mallavirus, and she had nursed each one to the end, expecting that her fate would be the same. She buried her mother, father and sister in the garden and waited for the symptoms of fever to appear in her own body. They did not. Lonely and grieving, she did her share of looting to stay alive, waiting for the madness to end. It didn't. Trapped in the urban jungle of sickness and violence, she made her escape to the countryside. Village after village chased her away, fearful of contamination. Food was scarce, no one would take her in. She went back to the town and sold her body for food. It was not even an existence. A member of the Waldenby gang took a liking to her, and she made the journey with him to the house where she immediately became public property. She had no dreams. She just wanted it all to stop.

Barwin, who definitely had a dream, told them about her island. She told them the story in her mind about the beautiful isolated land untouched by the mobs, ignored by the corporations and bursting with fruit and edibles of every kind. Where the water ran pure from unpolluted mountain streams and it was impossible not to be healthy. An island where birds and animals were unmolested by humans, where she would have a family of many children who would grow up happily in the privilege of total freedom. It was a fairyland, she knew, but the happy thought was infectious enough to stir the spirits of those who had known such hardships.

Fortune had tossed each of them a half-smile from time to time, and they had grasped it, improvised, and stayed alive. Always the unknown lurked, often maleficent, sometimes fortuitous, and still they had travelled on. The human capacity for hope to motivate and energise the struggle for a sustainable outcome transcends belief and optimism. In the case of this diverse group, hope beyond the ordinary was needed to obliviate the horrors of the recent past.

The river ran south. They had given themselves completely over to its whim. And as a new dawn painstakingly struggled to assert itself over the night sky, the silver-grey reflections on the water revealed that the burgeoning river had ripened into a mature body of water. The little boat was drifting in the central current which itself was churning more lazily than before. A low haze blocked the sunrise for a time, but they could just make out that the still grey banks of the river were much further away.

They shuffled themselves around to ease the stiffness of the night in their bones.

"Carefully now, don't sit on the eggs," said a watchful Artan.

Barwin looked at him in wonder. They had eggs! She hadn't seen an egg in more than a year. He smiled his self-conscious smile back to her. Happy that his forethought was properly understood. For eggs, if fertilised, would be a magnificent lifeline to take them into the future. Blue and Adam understood less well. Their existence to date had not compounded them to think of long-term planning. For them eggs were for eating. The ancient paradox of which came first, the chicken or the egg, was at least clear in this case. It was the egg. Indeed, it always had been the egg.

Whether these eggs would yield chickens or not was a much more important question.

They set about an incubation programme. It would take about three weeks of careful temperature control and constant turning for there to be a success. Adam was enthralled by the idea and immediately took ownership of the job. He unpacked the rudimentary straw nest Artan had made in a scrap of sacking and repacked it, carefully turning the eggs round as instructed. It might be a problem to keep the temperature up at night, so he looked round for more insulation, and his eyes alighted on Barwin's cascades of long unruly hair.

She couldn't think of a better use for it, so they sawed through the tousled inches with a knife and wrapped each egg carefully in a cushion of bright hair, sat it in the straw and sacking, then decided that Barwin's cap would make the perfect nest.

Short red hair suited her. It was still unruly.

The wooden boat glided gently as if it was on a stage, and someone unseen was rolling the scenery past. Sitting, watching, absorbing the light and the scuttling creatures along the riverbanks, the moorland had already changed into forgotten fields. The beauty of their abandonment was soon to be realised, for they were turning green. Unmolested and ungrazed, the power of the natural world was reasserting herself. All that was needed was an absence of land management, and of course the right weather conditions.

The scenic splendour rolled past, and they sat breathless, enjoying the panoramic show. Trees long thought dead were breaking out of their droughty hibernation and sprouting little shoots here and there. Sometimes from the ground level, sometimes from a branch which has held its courage and not capitulated to the despair of its comrades.

A roe deer, small and elegant in its coat of reddish brown and little white chin looked up at them as they passed, then dipped its head once more to the water to drink. The beauty of the scene hit Adam the hardest. Clutching the eggs to his chest, he cried.

The sobbing was contagious. They all cried, releasing the torments of the past, the raw emotions, shocks, the loss of Ellie and Nina. Tears of intense unexpected emotion. Terrible and wonderful at the same time. Tears of sorrow. Tears of relief. Beautiful healing tears to mingle with the water in the river and carry their sadness away.

Artan, ever the forward-thinking improviser, had been dragging a line through the river in the hope of catching a fish. He had prepared it with a tuft of hen's feather secured to some rusty remains of barbed wire. The line had trailed casually from the boat all night, but now, suddenly, he saw it twitch.

They all moved around, rocking the boat unsteadily to look. Artan gently, so gently, pulled the line a little. He held his breath. It could be anything. Pulling it in a bit more, he felt the twitch again. Heart beating faster, for they had no food on board, he reeled the line in, desperately aware that whatever he had caught might not be securely hooked.

A quick flash of water and he knew it was a fish. He stood up and skilfully yanked the struggling swish of silver into the boat. Not pausing to congratulate himself, he quickly sliced off its head, silently thanking it as he did, just as his mother had taught.

It was time to make for the banks, stretch their legs, clean themselves and make lunch. The river occasionally gave way to little sandy beaches, so all hands in the water to paddle, and using the branch as a rudimentary oar and pole, they slowly made their way to the nearest bank.

The girls couldn't wait to get into the water and wash the repugnant remains of their recent experiences away; they jumped in before Artan could secure the boat. Adam, still clutching his precious eggs, sat stock still on the boards, almost afraid to move in case some untoward event might dislodge his charges from his grip, for in his mind they were already hatched and cheeping away in some imagined land called paradise.

The cool clear water bathed away the final vestiges of Barwin's hideous experience. With Blue it was not so easy. She had half a lifetime of ugly encounters to scrub out of her, and still there was the baby, growing steadily inside, a constant reminder of the mixed feelings she would hold for many months. Her heart burned back to another time, and tender thoughts of the man who should have been the father to this child, the man lost in the streets of gang warfare, a lifetime ago, a man to whom she would silently dedicate all the future paradise moments of her life, for she was Blue by name and, now, after all had been lived through, blue by nature. Living had been too high a price to pay.

Artan the stoic set about gathering fuel for a fire. A small stream ran into the river, and along its banks he discovered the same kind of water cress which grew and thrived in the Valley. He picked some as a nutritious accompaniment to the fish, and some he wrapped in dampened tree bark to take with them, wherever they were going. And that at least was one thing held firmly in the hands of destiny.

They camped and ate in this clean quiet place for some days, but it was not a permanent arrangement. Too open, no cover, no protection from the inevitable next storm, no form of fortification, and probably too prone to flooding. They discussed it and agreed. Time to move on.

And they would move on again and again, passing silently through decaying cities harbouring only the moan of the wind, passing through the shadows of glass skyscrapers, eerie, empty, deserted even by the hubris which built them. A few ducks and geese inhabited the once proud lawns of the rich, signally the beginnings of a pastoral life. The freshness in the air, the darkness of the night, heightened their sense of how different it all was now, now the age of the human was diminished. No one needed a city any more.

Already the hardy buddleia was sprouting from the cracks in bridges. Thin grasses were going to seed in the window boxes of abandoned country inns. Trees dead and strewn along the pavements gave rise to homes for mosses and scuttling insects. The dawning of a new, hopeful age was being witnessed by these few watchers silently sliding through the ages of yesterday, silently watching as history faded behind them, and they knew they were peeping solicitously at the dawn of a brave new age, an age of green.

One afternoon when they were sitting on the remains of an old jetty, trying for a fish or two, Adam looked up in a state of high agitation. He had nurtured his hopeful clutch of eggs with all the care of an expectant mother, giving them up only for short periods when he bathed or helped with the common chores of gathering wood and eatables.

"Something's happening!"

He had felt a tiny peck on his chest. Everyone gathered round as if a king was to be born.

Untying his chequered papoose, they witnessed the beautiful birth of one minute beak sticking out of a speckledy brown shell. They rejoiced. The eggs were fertile. Just one of each sex would be enough. He covered his incubating bundle quickly back up again.

"We'll need something to keep them in, to protect them," he said, almost clucking with excitement. "And what do they eat? We have to find them some food."

To quell Adam's rising panic, they moored up to scout out the centre of a city. The cathedral already crumbling, roof ripped asunder, the sandstone statues stared passive as if they'd seen it all before, and it didn't matter to them because another day, in the far future, they, or a likeness to them, would again grace the walls of a similar structure. What or who the god might be was of equal indifference to them.

It was decided to leave Artan with the boat. He had lived a life sheltered from the predatory creep of the Mallavirus, and might therefore be susceptible. Now was not the time to take unnecessary risks, especially when it could be avoided. Having never entered a city before, he was understandably a bit disappointed, but the wisdom of this decision was unassailable, so Barwin, Blue and Adam struck out to gather what useful materials they could.

The City

There was not much of the city to scavenge. The pathetic shrapnel of human intervention was reduced to supermarket baskets scattered here and there, blocks of cement broken up, a few pipes hanging out of walls, the wire and glass fibre conduits of a sophisticated communications system frayed and perplexed. Battered equestrian statues of the great and barely good listed drunkenly on their heroic plinths. How great thou art. Who bows in humble adoration? Only the plastic detritus of two worthless generations hung around long enough to answer.

They talked in hushed tones as they walked through the city streets. It was like a morgue. The empty buildings echoed to the sound of their footsteps. Glass and concrete rose out of the ground. Gone were the office workers, gone was the busy heave of commerce which made the city once so prosperous, and all on the back of destruction no matter which way you looked at it.

These once hallowed offices used to dance to the tune of oil tankers crossing the globe, the destruction of tropical forests, the coerced labour in far-off fields picking tea and coffee for distribution in billions of plastic cups – milk added by courtesy of the slave cows who never ate a blade of grass. The tills had rung to the sound of drugs distributed at great profit by the pharmaceutical industries, everything properly tested on captive animals who suffered pain beyond endurance so that humans could control the incessant depression which blighted the minds of low-paid workers and the unemployable unemployed cast unceremoniously into the dungeons of despair.

Banks raided the accounts of innocent people to prop up their misdoings, invested in weapons which tore a million bodies apart, laundered money from the drugs barons and failed to fail when their bubbles of mismanagement burst. It was an illusion of prosperity, and when the prosperity dissolved, all that was left was the smoke and shattered mirrors of a civilization built on debt, the greatest debtee of all being the law of nature, and she had come to collect.

A sign swung limply above a small shop. 'Paradise Café' it said. The irony was palpable, and you could slap your thighs with mirth if everything was not so deathly quiet, if it wasn't all so incredibly sad, if it hadn't all been so entirely preventable.

The seeds of destruction were sown the day the first steam engine belched into life. Ironically it was devised to pump water out of coal mines, making more coal more available. They burned coal to mine more coal to be burned, and the circle widened as the engine was put on wheels so that more coal could be transported for even more burning. The steam engine was a wonderful thing as an interim path to progress, but instead of using the technology to develop cleaner energy, mining became the fashion, and the earth was raided for more. Mined oil and gas became the energy of the future, and at the same time it compromised the future. The oil companies became huge, their investments too colossal to backtrack on, and in the accounting analysis, a return on investment was more important than any living thing.

The commerce upon which the city was built crashed faster than a falling tree, the damage to the fragile atmosphere did the rest. It had taken only three degrees of warming to turn the busy commercial world into an empty skeleton of man-made grief.

Only the Paradise Café lent a hint to the mind-set of the time. Maybe it had been a kind of utopia, built on the false promises of trade and taxes, but the mighty had fallen, poor things, thinking they had built a solid empire, discovering they had built little more than a house of cards.

Not even a scrap of paper remained to blow listlessly through the ominous streets. Turning a corner, they heard voices. The city had not been completely deserted, though why anyone wanted to remain was open to debate. They ducked into a smashed-up doorway to observe without being seen. There was a fight going on. A raggedy bunch of people were throwing missiles at another raggedy bunch of people. It was not clear what they were scuffling over.

Then another bunch of people came from a tangential street, the leader of which seemed to have some authority, or had assumed some authority, because he had on his head the remains of a pig's head, and several others, enough to outnumber the two scrapping bunches of rags, were following him.

He looked to be tall, although the pig's head made him look taller, and was comparatively smartly dressed. When his presence was noticed, the other two gangs ran off in opposite directions. The pig man had the overall demeanour of a person who was the street authority – mean, rough, and surly. He wore a pig's head as a bishop wears his mitre; stance erect, attitude hubristic; manner blithe and condescending. The pernicious bond of church and state not dead, not forgotten.

Barwin, Blue and Artan shrank back further. After their experience at Waldenby, they had no wish to get involved with these sorts of mean- looking people, but the pigs head was heading straight up the street where they were hiding.

They were in the doorway of what once had been a classy retail emporium. Broken glass everywhere, ripped up tiles, dismembered mannequins lying contorted on the ground. Without the expensive shiny lights which would have bedazzled long-ago shoppers, it was dark and foreboding. If only people had seen past the shiny lights in the first place, things might have turned out better.

You cannot walk on broken glass in silence. They painstakingly crunched their way into the dark, looking for something to hide behind. Voices could be heard coming nearer. Tensely they motioned to each other and stopped where they were. There was not a clear piece of floor anywhere, everything made some kind of noise. They held their breath, knives drawn, unable to see each other or what was going on outside.

More used to being on the run than imitating a statue, Barwin shifted her weight at the top of some stairs, just teeny-weeny bit. It was enough to create a tinkling noise, which unfortunately set off another tinkling noise as pieces of glass and mirror rearranged themselves, some falling down the flight of shallow stairs, setting off a chain reaction which lasted for interminably long seconds as piece after piece chinked in a terrifying melody across the silent halls.

Outside, the man wearing the pig's head motioned for one of his crew to investigate.

"Probably a rat," said the investigator.

"Can't be a rat, we've eaten them all," came the swift retort.

"There's always one," said another.

They heard him crunching clumsily across the floor and kicking the broken remains of smashed shop counters and mannequins as he went. He looked towards the gloom and sniffed; years of hunting through the urban jungle had enhanced his senses. He could tell something was there.

Returning to the doorway, he barked an order. "Stake out this place, when it comes out, we'll get it," and two men did as bid.

It was easy for Barwin to weigh the situation and decide what to do. Blue was pregnant, Adam was delicate. There was probably a back way out, but they would make too much noise finding it, so she replaced her knife in the belt under her jacket, and walked boldly to the door.

"Hello," she said inquiringly.

The two men spun round excitedly.

"I'm lost," she tried, hoping to dissolve any sense of threat they might have had.

They grabbed her, one on each side. "Didn't know we'd be trophy hunting today, did we."

Gross laughter ensued. She was marched up the road to where the rest of this gang were just going out of sight.

It was déjà vu for Barwin. Captured again. Men again. Same scenario, different place.

Her captors called out to the group in the distance in a childish sing-song voice. "Look what we've got." There was a high sense of congratulation as they all came to look at her. Pushing her around.

"Leave her alone," commanded the man in the pig's head.

They stepped back. He seemed to have absolute authority.

"Take her to the station, and look around for any more like her."

The two original captors marched her to a disused railway station not far away. She noted the buildings and streets she passed. It would be far easier to track back in the city than the countryside.

The building was old but well organised. She was taken through the machine shop where a few men and women were working away building mechanical parts for unknown use, at least to her. There was a sense of industry about the place, and for once she got the feeling that some people actually knew what they were doing.

Passing the scene, she was taken to a small room, possibly the manager's office. There were assorted papers on the desk. She stared at the paper. She hadn't seen paper for years.

A woman came in. Short and officious, she sat down at the desk.

If Barwin had expected a greeting, she was disappointed.

"What skills do you have?"

Barwin racked her brain for something useful. "I can read and write. I am strong. I can grow food. I'm a fast learner."

It seemed a bit empty. She wanted to be an engineer.

"We are making windmills. There is a shortage of skills. Is there anything else you can do?"

Barwin was impressed. Finally someone had come to their senses and started to think about the future, though at this stage she didn't know how she could be part of it.

The officious woman took the silence to mean that Barwin had nothing to add.

"She's young and strong. Put her on handcar loading. We'll train her up on something more useful later."

Barwin was led out to the back of the station where the rails were laid out. Perched on some of the metal tracks in orderly queues were a selection of wheeled carts. One came by. It was being pumped up and down by four people operating a lever in a see-saw action. On the trolley were boxes of assorted tools and vegetables.

In the absence of fossil energy like oil, the combustion engine had become quickly useless. In the absence of an electricity grid, even renewable energy became untenable except for very small-scale producers such had once been at Waldenby. However, human power was reasonably plentiful. Hand-operated rail carts had been around as long as the rails, the design was there, it just needed a few railway parts and a touch of ingenuity to remake the old idea and bring some rudimentary communication back into operation.

As she looked in some slight awe at the organisation of the place, she heard a kerfuffle going on across the far side of the half-dozen or so tracks. People were arguing, standing in a half-circle around a man. The man in the pig's head was sitting calmly, watching and listening. The man in the middle was remonstrating. Barwin thought it looked like a court of some sort, and not the sort of court she would like to get involved with. The man was pleading, people were pointing at him, voices were raised. Then the man in the pig's head stood up, aimed a gun and shot him dead.

None of the people around her had looked up to witness the scene. In fact, they all kept their heads exceedingly low.

"Never get involved," whispered a woman next to her.

Everyone looked jittery, work- rates increased, no one spoke. Every single person had suddenly found quite a lot to do as they tried to confine their nervousness.

The pig man had got his name because of the pigs he had found on the outskirts of the city. He had captured them and reared them, guarded them and protected them, expanding his herd all the time. Finding these pigs and rearing their offspring was a great boon to all when there was practically nothing left to eat. But this man would watch people starve rather than give up a slice of pig in the early days.

He was a canny man. Early in the looting he had stockpiled guns and ammunition, deciding a mode of defence or attack was at least as important as food. Anyone trying to steal a pig from this man would be shot on sight. He took no prisoners.

Pigs grow quickly and can eat most things. They were an ideal commodity. But as the traditional means of exchange or barter dried up, the pig man discovered another form of payment. Enslavement. If people wanted to eat, they must do what he wanted them to do, or they would die – either by the gun or starvation. A debt-based society replaced by a fear-based society. It was difficult to see how things could work out otherwise. Catastrophic societal breakdown had always given birth to tyrants, yet it was the tyranny of the corporations, backed up by the governments they had bought, which caused the social unrest in the first place. The large corporations had wittingly caused climate change, which had released the Mallavirus, spawned the hurricanes and enabled the conditions for starvation. The cycle of tyranny continued, sometimes wearing a mask, sometimes not.

In this way the pig man had conquered his corner of the city. His body guards were well looked after – although notionally enslaved, and everyone under his control had to witness the execution of detractors as often as possible. Fear equalled control equalled fear. A tidy equation.

The pig herd having grown to a sustainable enough size, he next decided that although food brought some power, energy could bring more. Thus he commandeered the train shed and started to collect tools and machinery in order to construct his next project, which was to be a windmill. He had no appropriate skills himself, so recruiting the right skills was paramount. His engineers readily made use of defunct train carriages to make the human-propelled carts, and two birds were killed with one stone. He could increase his market range for pig meat, and he could at the same time send out search parties to press-gang more human labour.

He gambled that in a few years the land would recover from the excesses of over production and nutrient deficiency, and although climate change would be a challenge for perhaps hundreds of years, others would find new ways of producing food, and his monopoly would be over. Energy would be the next big thing. He was about to make sure his people would construct many windmills, and he alone would control the power, finger on the button, so to speak.

Barwin didn't go to the school of meek, and quickly reconnoitred the area with her eyes. She would try to leave as soon as an opportunity presented itself. The others could only wait for her for as long as it was safe for them to do so, and looking at the way these people operated, especially the pig man, no one was likely to be safe for long.

"Why don't you run away?" whispered Barwin to the woman moving some containers near her. The one who had muttered the quiet warning to her earlier.

"Not worth it, there'd be a bounty on my head. Anyway, nowhere to go, dear, my family are all here."

"Where's the weak point?" tried Barwin, but the woman just moved away.

Barwin was given a job loading up the next handcar with bits of old metal, and the next. She worked all morning loading and unloading, watching, listening.

The sensible way out was on a handcar, straight down the rails, but she wasn't on one. Randomly making a run for it was too risky.

Then came a break when everyone in the yard went over to a corner for a drink of water. Barwin tied her grungy scarf tight over her bright hair. If she could get lost in the crowd, it might make it easier for her to make a break.

Eyes darting everywhere, she looked for an opening, anything. The yard was guarded by armed men and women. They looked mean. The tracks were too open, the machine room was guarded too.

She sidled up to a man in the crowd. "Where do we go after work?"

He chuckled. "There is no after work. We sleep over there," he said, pointing to another railway shed across the lines.

She supposed that would be guarded too.

Daylight faded. The working people were herded across the lines to the other shed where they abluted in a foul-smelling washroom. Then led into a compartmentalised dormitory. Some compartments were big, for families, some were smaller. Some chatter broke out and children arrived to be reunited with their parents. All children were put into training at the earliest opportunity. The skills needed were plentiful, and each child was appointed a skill according to the intelligence assessments laid out.

After some food - mostly pork - they were allowed to ablute once more, then, as the light faded, they were shut into their compartments. Barwin was sharing a bunk with a middle-aged woman who tended to mutter to herself, and who also snored. The woman wasn't at all in the mood to converse, she just looked through Barwin and muttered about something to a person who wasn't there. It was to do with her family, children possibly, brothers possibly. Whoever they were they surely kept her company, and Barwin awake.

The plan Barwin hatched that night, or at least the most hopeful plan she could think of, was to find a drain in the washroom and get into it. The drain hopefully led to the river.

A thin dawn light signalled the time for everyone to rise. There was pork and porridge for breakfast, and certainly not enough to get fat on – if you could stomach enough of the stuff to actually get fat on it.

Barwin watched the slow movements to the washroom, and followed, eyes glued to the floor. There were no obvious drain covers, but she had the feeling that the squarish pieces of metal hammered into the ground in various parts of the building probably hid access points. The toilets did not flush as such, but emptied into some kind of hole; what happened next was anyone's guess, but it was bound to be unpleasant.

She paced as nonchalantly as she could, listening all the while to the sounds her feet made on the metal covers, until she found one which seemed looser than the others, and tipped at the corner of it with her boot to check its integrity. A loose corner was one thing, lifting the whole thing up in order to get a body through would be quite another. She supposed the stench might suffocate her.

Raised voices came from the sleeping quarters. She could tell there was something unusual going on because normally people were very quiet for fear of drawing attention to themselves. She imagined that she was not the only one looking for a way out of here, but in a climate of fear and control absolute, they would probably most likely be loners like her. She didn't have time to make alliances.

The raised voices were turning into a commotion. People were leaving the washroom to find out what was happening. She had to make her move quickly. Smiling at the two or three people who remained, she hauled up the metal plate to make her move. It was too heavy. She hauled at it with all the strength she could muster, and simply could not get under it at the same time as holding it up. Seeing what she was doing, two of the other women looked meaningfully at each other, rushed over, and pulled it up for her. She took a deep, deep breath and was gone. The metal plate slammed down over her head.

If she had tried to calculate how far she would fall, she would have been wrong. She did not fall far, it was what she fell into which surprised her. Clearly she knew the substance of what she would land in – faeces – but she didn't know, nor could she know, that she was waist-deep in a cesspit which had been dug out under the washroom, and that the drain outlets had been blocked up.

The cesspit was shovelled out regularly. Human waste in this form was a valuable commodity. It could be taken away and composted, then spread or dug into the land as a nutrient-rich fertilizer. It was entirely logical that the pig man would not waste this useful resource; what was illogical was that millions of humans, in a previous life, did. In a previous life people spent vast amounts of money on synthetic fertilizers, which grew plants all right, but did nothing to sustain the soil. Worse, they contaminated ground water, stayed in the soil for decades and the run-off killed fish. It was just another madness prolonged by the big marketing machines who cared nothing for the land or the water. They were just another link in the chain of destruction. Profit they could make, and profit they would.

The stench from the methane and sulphurous gases made Barwin gag. Once landed, she quickly looked for an escape route, knowing she could be asphyxiated at any moment. She made for the blocked-up holes where the drain exits might have been. The job was a botch. Just pieces of board roughly tacked into place. With only minutes in which to make a decision, she went for a board which was about her size. She pulled at it. It didn't move. A shovel was hanging on the wall over the door which was probably used as an access point for emptying the cesspit. She had to wade and practically swim through the sludge to get it, lungs bursting. Then wade back again. Terrified to take a breath, she almost exploded her lungs trying to lever the board off. It gave. She threw herself at the opening, gasping for breath, and crawled down the filthy pipe as fast as she could.

Only liquids had seeped through to this drain. The air was not a lot fresher, but she scraped and crawled her way until she simply had to stop from exhaustion. It was an old sewer, cracked and cobwebby. In places the cobwebs were as thick as a curtain. Stopping to regain her breath and her sense of direction, she deduced from the direction of the foul water running beneath her that the drain was gently sloping downhill. Moving on more slowly, she noticed smaller drains emptying into this one; they were fairly clean and probably out of use. She looked for an inspection manhole going up from the road, and a small chink of light intimated that there was one. Groping for the curved metal step irons which acted as a ladder, she pulled at the lowest one. It came away from the wall in her hand. She reached for the next, that held. Gingerly she made her way up the rotting structure to street level and listened for any signs of activity. It was quiet. The manhole cover was incredibly heavy, and as she shouldered it, another step iron came out of the wall in her hand, almost making her fall. She clung on, and wedged the broken piece of iron into a gap, rested, then worked the broken iron around the manhole. Terrified that once she moved it she would be greeted with a kick in the face or worse, she paused for a few minutes, ears keen to pick up any noise at all. Luck was on her side. A huge heave and her hand was out, then her shoulder, then a knee, and she hauled her body out, eyes everywhere. Luck was holding. She rolled to the gutter, paused, then rolled to the cover of a building. Then she saw the muddy banks near the river.

It wasn't the place where they had left the boat, but it would do. Bent over double she half-crawled, half-ran to the bank and threw herself into the water.

The current caught her. It dragged her downstream. She gasped at the comparative cold of the water and looked for the boat. She didn't recognise the banks. Either she was too far upstream or too far downstream. Upstream, she hoped.

Drifting past the cityscape was like living the end of a dream. She relaxed, and let the water carry her along, further to the middle now. Maybe the others had had to leave. They wouldn't abandon the boat. The thought of a watery grave entered her mind. At least it was clean water, unpolluted by the toxins of industry and human excrement. Unconcerned, she noticed she was drifting towards a bridge, a road bridge, defunct, to all intents and purposes with its once proud array of steel wire and concrete stanchions, yet another symbol of the catastrophic industrial past. She lazily wondered how many hundreds of years would have to go by before another such edifice was built. Peddling her arms to keep her head above water, she wondered if it had been worth surviving the catastrophe. A glimpse of the last few years caroused through her mind in just a few seconds. One always asks why. Why did she make it this far, only to fall in a river and drown.

The foreboding shadows of the bridge felt like death itself. Bleak, dark, and cold. The current took her past the supports under the roadway and back into the light. Maybe she heard a shout, but she was getting too tired to turn around. It had been a long day.

The branch of a tree landed in front of her. She grabbed it automatically, as a drowning man does. Then something bumped into her, or was it an arm.

Blue, Artan and Adam had taken the boat to the shadows under the bridge in order to hide, and wait, as long as they could. Keen as they were to go and retrieve one of their number from an unknown fate, they also knew that to imperil three for the sake of one was bad odds. There was little choice other than to do exactly what Barwin would have wanted them to do, and to trust her to escape, or abandon her if the situation demanded it.

Adam caught Barwin by the arm and dragged her unceremoniously into the boat. It was fortunate the water had washed most of the filth from her, or they might well have flung her back in.

The Storm

All that had come before was to be irredeemably lost in time. Maybe archaeologists of the future would come and dig it all up again, piecing it back together for another generation, making up stories which didn't exist. Maybe they would write about a lost civilization, maybe they would get it all wrong and blame the demise of the Anthropocene on a natural disaster, or a meteorite, or an invasion of evil aliens. Maybe they would get it right. But they wouldn't learn the lesson. From ancient Ur to the twenty-first Century calamity in the River Jordan, humanity had shot itself in the proverbial foot thinking it could bind the laws of nature to its will. Piling failed strategy onto failed strategy, local disasters had paved the way to regional disasters. It would not take so very long for them to turn global. More human interference was employed to try and put it right. Nowhere was there the patience or the will to simply stand back and let the land recover on its own, as it surely would. Patience doesn't increase GDP, disasters do.

Still they drifted on, for no place they visited was home. Past the sunken graveyards of abandoned nuclear power stations, their toxic legacy of contamination seeping slowly though the water-table to compromise the genetic structure of all living things. Fish, bird and the unwise sapiens; forever modified; life-spans diminished. Some would mutate, some would not. Future Darwinists sketching out their trees of life might wonder at the perfunctory stump at the end of the line.

They drifted faster now in the outgoing tide, past the decay of the coastal belt where the foundations of smashed buildings stuck out of the estuarial mud like glooping burial chambers. The crumbling chimneys of coal-fired power stations stood as a final worthless salute to a defunct society based on an insatiable desire for the very energy which was to engender its collapse.

The once proud seafaring nation was reduced to the rusting hulks of washed up boats and cargo ships lying dismembered on the rocks. The sea no longer a tributary for trade and wealth, only the foolhardy ventured upon it. Smashed metal containers, their doors prised open, lie prostrate on the mud, their contents of worldly goods rich pickings for the coastal scavengers. But even that time was gone. If you came down to the shifting shore you made sure you had a quick escape route, because the blurred place between land and sea was a dangerous place. Storms could come without warning. The shipping forecast beloved of mariners and landlubbers alike had melted into the electromagnetic radiation of radio waves from which it was born. They said only a nuclear holocaust would stop transmission of public service broadcasting. How clever everybody had been to worry about the wrong thing.

And under the sea the bright yellow containers of nuclear waste liquids and solids with a destructive half-life of twenty-four thousand years rolled along with the ocean churn, splitting and leaking, ensuring that even a life after climate change would be blackened by the greed and thoughtlessness of the human species.

The insatiable desire to burn for energy had caused so much pain. The ice caps were all but gone, the rising sea had swallowed entire cities along with the humble and innocent islands which did nothing to deserve their fate. Mallavirus had taken millions of lives in agony. Only the birds' nests of plastic junk piled high on the encroaching shoreline would last long enough to count the dead. Alas, there were few birds to use even these.

And all the while the air pressure was dropping.

The river had emptied them into an unruly estuary and the current took them south-west. In the far distance Artan saw the ominous darkness in the sky.

They had had their weeks of perfect weather, knowing only the soft breeze on the river which barely moved the grasses on the banks. In that time they lived and played as children, getting to know each other, hunting and catching food, gathering plants and making rudimentary oars and rudder to ease their way. The sturdy boat had given them so much joy and independence that they were forgetting the other side of the coin.

It was coming from the north-west, the storm, coming from the direction of the Valley. Yet Artan looked at it passively. He could do nothing for his mother; Ben was there in any case. But he must do something for the contents of this boat. They had got sloppy. Nothing was particularly well anchored or tied down. Explaining the possibilities to the others, they set themselves to the vital task of ensuring their cargo of plants and cuttings and six yellow fluffy chicks were lashed down well enough to withstand what they all dreaded.

The wind started its familiar whirl, and they each tied themselves to a section of boat. Adam tied himself to Blue and the chicks as well, warm and safe enough in their wire baskets and layers of polythene.

One hadn't hatched, but he doggedly cocooned it just the same.

Livid sky, choppy waters. You could read the weather runes with your eyes closed. When every day could be your last, what is another last day.

They settled down in the boat to chat, about nothing and everything. About the place they would settle in and the sort of community they dreamed of.

"No special hats," said Barwin, who was highly suspicious of anyone who had to wear a special hat to claim their authority, the pig man still fresh in her mind.

"No money!"

"No fences and no borders!"

"No religion," yelled Blue, who had torn herself apart trying to reconcile her strict Catholic upbringing with her existential need to barter her body.

The swell of the sea intensified, and the small craft rose and fell on the gathering strength of the angry waves.

"We must have peanut butter!" laughed Blue, shouting against the wind. "I'm pregnant and I need peanut butter!"

In the madness of the moment they all caught her mood. She had been morose about the baby, not quite in denial, but understandably reluctant to talk about it. Now, in what might as well be the final reckoning, for none of them expected to survive, here she was embracing her pregnancy with gusto. If feelings of relief were possible in that watery inferno, they surfaced in smiles. Smiles all round. Spiritual peace descended and calmed the waters of their frightened minds. The bittersweet song of end-times redemption.

It was time to laugh and sing. Everything was out of their hands. They made up the words to songs they did not know, and hung on to the slippery wet sides of the boat as waves as high as houses tossed them about like the toys of a belligerent toddler. They sang and roared and shouted their obstinate refusal to be cowed until they could no longer hear themselves, and still they fought in mental ferociousness, obstinately refusing to cow to the insatiable greed of the storm.

The wind and waves took them in every direction and none. They did not know where they were going in the first place, so any place would do. Swirled every which way, now at the crest of a wave, now in a watery abyss, destruction imminent. The sickening swell and vertiginous swoop as they were swept up from dark valley to precarious mountain tops then lunged down again, and the little boat shook, absorbed the blow, one more time, again.

Rain and salty spume poured onto them faster than they could bail out. Four of them working double fast, triple fast, endlessly emptying of buckets and bowls whilst the falling waves beat crushing on their heads. They filled and refilled and swung the water overboard, and it just came in faster as if the spell of the Sorcerer's Apprentice had been re-cast in apocalyptic proportions.

And then it got no worse.

The wind began to subside. The waves still huge and indomitable continued their enormous swell in a universe of undulating sea. But it got no worse. The sea bickered with itself, simpering obsequiously in its argument with the wind which had dropped and changed direction.

The exhausted crew laughed and punched the air like drunken fools.

Still the water in the boat had to be emptied, still the danger was omnipresent, but the eye of the storm had passed them by.

Night descended on the exhausted occupants. Still tied to the boat, they let the degenerating swell lead the way, and fell into a fitful sleep.

"Worse things happen at sea," chuckled Barwin ruefully, and she realised she would never see her gran again.

The Island

They drifted for hours, and the endless ocean remembered its place in the order of things and calmed down. The sun beamed, burned.

They used the time to take stock of what they had left in the boat. Adam took a crushed, half-formed chick out of the papoose around his chest, and mourned. Some of their food was lost, and there was little drinking water left, but the yellow fluff of lives cheeping in the wire basket wrapped in copious layers of plastic had survived. Adam unwound them from the orange hair donated by Barwin, which had been their miracle cushion, and fed them some grass seeds and drops of water. Artan, despite Adam's protestations, used the dead chick for bait, and trailed a line for fish, and they anxiously scanned the horizon for land.

Whatever it was, they were drifting towards it. Just a black spot sticking out of the wide blue. A seagull on the wing, then another.

The warming temperature of the sea and land would always have winners, and gulls were among them. The migration of marine species from further south meant that their food supply continued to be abundant. Where there were gulls there was land, breeding grounds, eggs, guano, fertilizer, potential.

Drifting nearer, the small black spot became a big black spot, then an island, then daunting cliffs. They faced it with trepidation. A battered and leaking wooden dingy was no match for the determination of the current. Artan was frantically using the rudimentary rudder to try and steer round the island. Oars were plied on one side only to help swing the craft round. They would be smashed if they couldn't change course.

Artan struggled with the rudder, concentration and determination on his face. Adam picked up the seriousness of the situation, pulled up a bench seat and stabbed it into the water on the off-side to create drag. It didn't look as though they had enough time to clear the cliffs. Barwin and Blue unfolded the sheet of polythene which had protected the chicks and stretched it across the boat in the oncoming breeze to slow the boat further. They were buying time.

Slowly, slowly the little boat changed its course and nosed its way round the side of the island, edging perilously close to the jagged rocks scattered round the base of the cliffs. The waves dashed violently against them, rebounding across the cliffs to toss the wooden craft about in every direction. They pushed themselves back from the rocks with every instrument to hand, hearts stopping, the girls dropped the makeshift sail and readied themselves to jump.

A huge wave heaved at the boat, and Barwin was thrown into the writhing water, hurling both her and the craft back towards the rocks. Barwin surfaced, blinded by the water, and was trapped between the boat and the rocks. She pushed her hands against the boat and stabbed her feet towards the rock to try and absorb the impact. She barely felt the pain as her hips and back were crushed. But it had worked. The boat, carried back by the churn of the rebounding wave, was washed clear of the rocks.

And then it was over. The boat bobbed away from the brooding black of the cliffs and rounded the side of the island. The topography changed dramatically, and the churn of the sea diminished. From their new vantage point they could see that the land dropped quickly away and small beaches could be seen set between large rocky outcrops. There were caves large and small carved by the passing of eons of tide, wind and time. They rounded a small bluff and there, laid out before them in a perfect horseshoe, was a beautiful sandy lagoon of clear azure water.

The three dazed people in the boat stared in silent disbelief. Maybe they had died and gone to heaven. Small eddying currents gently manoeuvred them into the lagoon. Tall trees caught the eye and led up to low mountains in the distance; all was green, lush and mouth-wateringly edible. Birdcall emanated from the bushes nearby, small fish darted around the boat. They were almost afraid to get out.

Only when the rippling waves lapped the battered craft onto the grinding of silver sand did the spell break. They whispered to each other, afraid to disturb the magic of this wondrous alchemy. Unsure what to do. Light which had travelled for billions of years across the universe, uninterrupted since the dawn of time, glanced upon their skin, transmitting the pure energy of the first dawn around them. The cosmos seemed to smile. They felt its warmth and knew they had found home.

There is terrible wonder in finding that which you dream of, a sorrowing joy, that in finding your dream, you have nothing left to dream. Barwin felt herself floating onto the beach. Watching Artan and Blue drag the boat up above the high tide mark, watching Adam unpacking and clucking over the surviving chicks like a proud parent. For all the world he was Mother Adam, giving his children names, stroking their tiny heads, their profound innocence healing his mental scars. It would take a while, but

Adam would recover his generous loving self in this sanctuary of peace.

Blue stretched out on the warm sand, hand resting gently on her swelling belly. Her sorrowing trials retreating into the mist of past lives. Relaxed and happy, she hadn't dreamed of an island, she had lived beyond dreaming, even a void would have been preferable to the life she had been forced to endure. The sun kissed her legs and arms, and filled her with a depth of warmth and gratitude only a horribly abused person can feel. It was all over. Finally over. Adam brought her over a drink, and they sat close, chatting, heads almost touching, as close friends do.

Barwin struggled to absorb the moment.

There was overwhelming love in her as she gazed wistfully around the island. Even in her most tantalising dreams she had not imagined such beauty. She had become almost comfortable with uncertainty and accepted that the uncontrollable chaos of life was just that – life. She had secretly imagined a cabin by a stream on an island free from the greed of marauding gangs, and with enough wild food to sustain her small appetite. She had envisaged a co-operative of scattered people, each specialising in something and bartering their wares. She wanted to smell the scent of wildflowers and till unbroken land. It was a peaceful dream. It was a modest dream. She had never really thought through what she would do should it ever come true.

Nature had been generous when she spared this island. The trees still stood, the birds still sang. Possibly it was on the edge of the new hurricane belt. Possibly they had been driven far to the south where the changing conditions had arranged a subtropical microclimate. It had generous ponds of fresh water, fruit in the trees, berries and unhurried wildlife which moved slowly across the fertile ground and observed without fear.

Barwin had always followed her heart and her truth. Her sensitivity had been heightened by all that had happened, and a deeper understanding of the nature of all things became clear. The loveless greed of everything she had left behind, which had massacred so much of the land and sea, had ultimately laid waste to empathy in the human heart. This was her most profound lesson.

Evolution may not have depended on conscience and morality in the past, but that is not to say that the future would be the same. The empty spirit of capitalism without consequence had destroyed everything which it sought to have dominium over, and in the process had destroyed itself. The death it had been running away from had bared its teeth and turned to meet it, catastrophically.

There was only one love, and that was the harmonious coexistence of every living thing, from microorganism to mountain. Nature had pulled Barwin into its bosom by its very absence, and though nature was only sleeping, the slumber was enough to eradicate the perpetrators of her condition, the human.

She knew the others felt it too. She watched as they made their first camp among the mango trees, and started, at first tentatively, to develop a caring relationship with everything around them. The time to kill was over. Now they were custodians of the natural world. They would give to it, not take. Every bird, tree and stream became an object of love. Every living thing became part of their own blossoming spirit.

After a few days another small group of people walked to the outskirts of their camp. Hesitant, smiling, and bringing gifts, they sat down in an attitude of peace and exchanged a few harmonious words. It was good. Maybe these were two small tribes who needed each other, who could help each other. There was more than enough space for a hundred such tribes.

Freed from the struggle of her existential burden, Barwin watched as her friends became tall and strong, imbued with the health and vitality of the sun, the sea and the nutrition-rich diet. Existence became a joyful alliance between all who lived on this happy island. Improvisation became enrichment, and the long history of homo sapiens began a new chapter. Not just here, but in little pockets of fertility all over the small blue dot.

She looked across the garden to Artan. Theirs had been a connection strong enough to stir the heart, beyond a meeting of minds, it had been a deep soulful alliance. She gazed at him, and smiled as he bent down to cut the vegetables. She wanted to hold him in her heart, to take some memory of him with her. He would have been her man.

Looking far across the distorted wings of eternity, she could see her mother, her kind face. She somehow expected it. It was time for her to leave this beautiful place of fertile abundance. Barwin felt she had been given a glimpse of the real utopia, and all the possibilities for peace and harmony it could offer, so that she would know humanity had been given another chance.

She watched as a slim, tanned girl touched Artan's shoulder, and picked up the basket of fruit beside him. He looked up at her and smiled.

Her mother called silently, and standing close by she could make out the face of her father, all traces of the virus gone, and behind them stood the tall and gracious presence of the ancestors, welcoming her.

Epilogue

Adam and Lucy Blue (for that was the name Adam called her) developed a long and enduring partnership based on respect and understanding. Together they brought up the little girl born three months after they landed on the island. They called her Barwin.

Artan and a girl from the other tribe gave birth to a baby boy, one of many hardy and robust children they would produce together.

In the evening the family groups would sit round the fire and tell stories. The story of Barwin, the legendary barbarian was a constant favourite with the children. Through these stories they would always know how she sacrificed herself to give them their dreams. In their stories they were always careful to impart the tale of making too many people, for they wanted all generations in the future to know that to go forth and multiply was only sensible if you had more than enough natural resources.

No one else came to the island, and the two tribes existed alongside each other, collaborating on projects and sharing resources. They had learned the hard lessons of the old days, no money, no fences, no borders – and definitely no special hats.